Mademoiselle Giraud, My Wife

Mademoiselle Giraud, My Wife

Adolphe Belot

MINT EDITIONS

Mademoiselle Giraud, My Wife was first published in 1891.

This edition published by Mint Editions 2021.

ISBN 9781513295381 | E-ISBN 9781513295534

Published by Mint Editions®

 MINT
EDITIONS

minteditionbooks.com

Publishing Director: Jennifer Newens
Design & Production: Rachel Lopez Metzger
Project Manager: Micaela Clark
Translated By: Émile Zola
Typesetting: Westchester Publishing Services

Publisher's Announcement

The article announcing the abrupt interruption of *Mademoiselle Giraud's* adventure in the *Figaro* has given birth to certain imputations which the author wishes to refute.

"*Mademoiselle Giraud, My Wife*," rests on delicate ground it is true, but we have aimed to palliate the form, to avoid all ill-sounding expressions, all too vivid colorings, and all indiscreet details. The author has preferred to sin by too much obscurity than by too much clearness, and he is convinced should this novel happen to fall in the midst of young minds, it would remain enigmatic. As to persons accustomed to read between the lines and grasp the artful omissions, they cannot blame us for approaching a subject already touched upon by respected writers, and notably by Balzac. They could at most claim that certain questions should always remain in the dark and that it is dangerous to raise them. The author is not of this opinion, and that he may not repeat himself, he refers his readers to Chapter XV of this volume. If, after perusing the said passage, they are not convinced, they must admit, at least, that this book has been seriously written, and that it contains useful instructions.

M. Adolphe Belot has just published a work—"Mademoiselle Giraud, My Wife"—which has succeeded in attracting public attention, in these days of political excitement. This novel, it appears, has attained the enormous sale of thirty thousand copies. For more than a year, it is the only volume that has torn such a multitude of readers from the ever-increasing stream of journals that threaten the destruction of libraries.

Such a phenomenon is good to study. I have just read M. Belot's work, and I now understand the cause of its success. The public believed it had found food for its unwholesome curiosity. What it seeks in the alcove indiscretions of certain sheets, it has sought in the grave and revengeful book of the novelist. And whilst it devoured its sound and strong pages, which it vainly strove to soil by its appetite for scandal, it declared aloud that this work was a shame, affecting the inability of even pronouncing its title in the presence of women, almost accusing the author of speculating on the depraved tastes of the epoch.

I like clear declarations. The real truth is that, while contributing to the author's success, many persons have pronounced the big word immorality, so void of sense in literary matters. When the public now deigns to read one of our works, it seems to say: "We read you, but it is because you are profoundly obscene, and we love spicy stories." Soon success will become a crime, a criminal imputation to public modesty; we can no longer sell two thousand copies of a book without it being asked what hazardous description the writer has attempted in his novel, that two thousand persons should have bought it.

I have undertaken the task, after reading *"Mademoiselle Giraud,"* to absolve M. Belot of his success. It is necessary that some one should say to the public: "Ah! do not lower your voice; let us speak aloud of that book of which you are making a work that your wives and daughters hide under their pillows. Since we still guillotine in broad day-light, we may also publicly brand certain vices with a red-hot iron. Do you not see that you wickedly and stupidly make a shameless speculator of a moralist who has courageously pointed out one of the dangers of the education of young girls in boarding-schools?"

I know it is considered good taste to conceal vice, that virtue may be permitted to live without blushing. We really make virtue of a too weak constitution. It is because it is virtue that it may hear all.

However, let us have no hypocrisy. We are very learned nowadays. We content ourselves with whispering what we forbid moralists to brand publicly. M. Belot has not taught anything to anybody; he has disturbed no innocence, in relating the monstrous friendship of two old school-friends. That story is not new in our depraved society. The author's crime is simply to have troubled the quietude of people who preferred to relate the story in question behind closed doors, to seeing it freely circulated with all its avenging consequences. And, as if to punish him for tearing away the veil, they endeavor to make him expiate his audacity by lending him all the intentions of scandal that they place in his book.

Ah, well; no, you did not understand. M. Belot is not worthy of the success you have given him. Cease to hide his book; place it on all your tables, as our fathers placed the rods with which they chastised their children. And, if you have daughters, let your wife read this book before she separates herself from these dear creatures to send them away to school.

The drama is of a terrible simplicity. I dare relate it.

A young man, Adrien de C— falls in love with Paule Giraud, a tall brunette who gives him her hand with a strange smile. Paule has an old school friend, Berthe de B— with whom she maintains assiduous relations. This Bertha, a blonde with gray eyes and red lips, had made a marriage of inclination, so the world believed at least, but her husband left her, no one ever knew why, and the world blamed the husband who disdained to defend himself. When Madame de B— hears that Adrien wishes to marry her friend she tries to dissuade him from the marriage with a persistency and many mysterious glances, which should have made the young man reflect.

The marriage is celebrated, but Adrien cannot consummate it. Paule discourages her husband's loving attentions, having nothing to give him but a sisterly affection. Adrien then believes that Paule deceives him; he watches and follows her, and when he sees her furtively enter a strange house, when he expects to find her in the company of a lover, he finds her with Madame de B— whom he has forbidden her to see. Nothing enlightens him, however; he is blind to the friendship of these two women. Conquered in the struggle he maintains, he becomes distracted and flies without guessing what fatality weighs on him.

He does not penetrate the depth of this infamy until he meets Berthe's husband at Nice, the man who had deserted his wife and accepted the condemnation of the world. The ancient orgies have passed there; the leprosy of Lesbos has overtaken our wives. Adrien, terrified, wishes to tear Paule from her shame. He prevails on M. de B— to return to France and take his wife in one direction while he takes Paule in another. But Bertha does not release her prey; she rejoins her companion, and when later Adrien is called to Paule, he finds her dying of a terrible malady; he can only avenge her by aiding heaven to drown Berthe, the girl with eye of gold of whom Balzac caught a glimpse in a nightmare.

Such is the work. It is a Juvenal satire. Only, M. Belot is of extreme chastity of expressions. He has not the tartness of the poet; he has the clear and cold tone of the Judge who probes human monstrosities and applies the eternal laws of chastisement as an honest man. Everybody can read the work. It is the indictment of a crime; it is a session of the court of assizes, during which the depravity of society is exposed with such severity of word that no one thinks of blushing.

And the moral of the book is blinding. When Adrien attempts the salvation, the redemption of Paule, she says to him with tears in her voice: "It is the boarding-school that has been my ruin; it is that life in common with companions of my age. Tell mothers to keep their children near them, and not place them in the apprenticeship of vice."

The public may now give M. Belot's work the success it pleases. To me it is an act of honesty and courage.

Emile Zola

I

A certain night, between a Tuesday and a Wednesday of last February, saw that part of the Avenue Friedland, between Rue de Courcelles and l'Arc de Triomphe, in a state of extraordinary animation. In front of a brilliantly illuminated mansion of the renaissance style, equipages, livery carriages and simple fiacres constantly deposited hooded women, and men in overcoats. They hurriedly crossed the broad sidewalk that separated the street from the house; one panel of the gate opened before them, and a small negro in livery silently pointed to the dressing-rooms at the left.

A few minutes later the men in evening dress, the women in dominoes of all shades with black velvet masks over their faces, ascended the stairway with sculptured balustrade.

As they reached the first drawing-room, the former directed their steps toward a personage of between forty-five and fifty years of age, and bowed or shook hands with him. He was tall, thin, and wore a full beard—a blonde beard well known in the Parisian world. The latter approached a young man standing at the entrance of the drawing-room, exchanged a sign with him, murmured a name, raised the edge of their masks, and having thus made themselves known, glided into a large gallery hung with precious canvas where the friends of the house were already assembled.

One might have believed himself in the foyer of the opera on a ball night, but at the opera of other days; of which our fathers retain the remembrance, at that epoch when we could converse, laugh and amuse ourselves without turbulence or scandal; where intrigue flourished, where society women were not exposed to the hearing of coarse conversation, or to be victims of cynical brutalities; where the mob had not replaced the throng; where wit had not yet given place to boisterousness, a sad but, alas! consecrated expression.

A group of political, worldly and artistic celebrities pressed around the host, himself a subtle and delicate wit—too delicate perhaps for our days—a veritable gentleman of letters who carried in literature the penalty of his native distinction, of his worship for the Eighteenth century, a portrait *de la Tour* lost in the midst of the canvasses of our realistic epoch.

The women were in the minority in this reunion, and it would have been difficult to say to which class of society they belonged.

The Parisian world had perhaps sent its most seductive embassadresses: if the name of some "respected" married woman, of some *grande dame* was whispered, a fashionable *demi mondaine,* or an actress in vogue, also betrayed her incognito. At the end of the gallery, at the right, seated around an elegantly served table, were three theatrical women celebrated for their beauty.

One of them, who was preparing to play the role of a consumptive on one of our great stages, was recognizable by her white and satiny shoulders, her round and sensual chin, and her lips of incomparable freshness; the second, who was celebrated for her jewels and her intermittent love for a great comedian, had under the pretext of heat removed her mask, and she appeared in all her beauty; the third had retained her mask, but her charming personality betrayed itself in her gaze, a gaze so incendiary that when her house burnt last summer, her friend accused her of having set fire to it with her eyes.

To what kind of fete were these people invited? Could it be a ball? No orchestra invited dancing. A concert? The voices scarcely hushed, when an artist approached the piano. It was a fete without name, of a peculiar kind; a sort of masked reception.

After walking around the drawing-room several times, exchanging many bows and hand-shakings, trying discreetly to penetrate a few of the masks and stopping several times in front of the sideboard, a charming man of our acquaintance, a naval lieutenant in Paris on a leave of absence, approached the host and asked him if, perchance, he had in his wise solitude reserved a small corner for those unfortunate mortals who could not pass a whole night without smoking.

"Indeed, my dear monsieur," replied M. X—, "I have reserved the entire second floor. Cross the gallery, turn to the left, ascend the stairway, enter my study and you will find something to satisfy your vices on my desk."

"We shall be eternally grateful for your thoughtfulness," cried Camille V—, hastening to follow the host's directions.

His vices found numerous companions; a dozen smokers already occupied the study. The lieutenant took a cigar from a bronze vase on the chimney, and spying a vacant chair, made straight for it. He was nonchalantly stretched out for a few moments, his head thrown back on the cushion of the chair, his legs crossed, giving himself up entirely to the pleasure of his fragrant Havana, when he suddenly thought he distinguished a familiar face through the thick smoke that obscured the room. He arose, made two or three steps forward, looked more attentively, and recognized Adrien de C—, one of his old comrades at the preparatory school of Sainte-Barbe, who for two years had been his companion and neighbor in class and study.

He could not be mistaken; there were the same regular features, the same gentle half-veiled gaze, and thin lips concealed by a light moustache. But how pale was the face, so ruddy in other days, and how emaciated! Premature lines could be seen around the corners of the mouth, the hair was now gray, and a bluish circle extended under the eyes. Could fifteen years have made such ravages and wrought this change? "Can I be as changed as he?" thought Camille V— in alarm.

Mechanically he turned toward the mirror on the chimney, and after a short scrutiny he was satisfied that he had not grown as old as his school-mate.

"And yet," he said to himself, "he has not led such a rude and changeable existence as myself; he has not wandered over the world, suffered from heat and cold, lived in unhealthy climates, faced tempests—" He stopped a few moments, then resumed his reflections:

"Yes, but he may have encountered some great misfortune; moral sufferings have more effect on some men than physical sufferings. We know not what deceptions, what sorrow, anguish and despair fifteen years may bring."

Thus thinking, he had gradually approached his friend. Adrien de C— was lost in thought and did not see him approach, but raising his head suddenly, he recognized his friend and extended his two hands.

"What! I find you at last!" he cried. "What happiness! I was inquiring about you only a few days ago. As usual I was told that you were wandering around the world and despaired of ever seeing you again. Now fortune reunites us after so many years. I am so delighted."

They sat down side by side and enjoyed a long conversation; they had so many souvenirs to evoke, so many things to say; Adrien de C— never wearied of interrogating the marine officer; how he had obtained his grades, what dangers he had run, what struggles he had encountered! and took pleasure in listening to his friend's account of his long voyages.

These accounts seemed to divert his mind, and he was happy to live for a few moments in the life of his friends, that he might escape from his own sad thoughts.

"But tell me of yourself," said Camille V— abruptly interrupting his narrative.

"Of myself!" replied Adrien de C— in dismay; "Oh! no."

"What! I have told you all my secrets, and you will not confide in me!"

"My life contains nothing of interest. I contented myself by following the career for which I had prepared."

"And to follow it with brilliant success; that I have heard. But tell me of your adventures all this time; you must have some anecdote, some event, great or small, to tell me! I lately heard at Toulon that you have been married for two years. Are you happy, and have you any children?"

Adrien de C— quickly raised his head and looked at his friend in such a strange way, that Camille could not help exclaiming:

"Is not my question only natural? Have I wounded you?"

As Adrien de C— did not answer at once, the lieutenant seized his hand warmly and said:

"You suffer—you have some great sorrow! And to whom will you confide it if not to me?—was I not your only friend, your brother in other days? Though we have lived so long apart, we have not ceased to love each other. Have you forgotten the pleasure we experienced in meeting? A glance sufficed for a recognition notwithstanding our long separation, and our hearts attracted us toward each other before our hands clasped."

"Ah! why did I not meet you sooner," replied Adrien sadly. "You would have aided me with your advice, you would perhaps have consoled me. Now nothing can be done, and I have nothing to say."

And as if fearing new questions and new prayers, he arose and drew his friend toward the drawing-room.

The scene had greatly changed since the lieutenant left it. More animation and gayety reigned. After the supper, a few had removed their masks, and many pretty faces were revealed. Others allowed their identity to be guessed. Shoulders, understanding they had a duty to fulfill, little by little threw off the cloaks that covered them and appeared in all their enticing beauty.

The host, unable to resist any longer the pressing solicitations, had changed the program of the fete and permitted a few waltzes and quadrilles.

Laughter had succeeded conversation, and dancing had replaced intrigue. It was no longer a reception but a ball, all the more animated for having commenced so late, and because an infinity of pretty feet had to take a glowing revenge for their long inaction.

The two friends walked around the drawing-room for a last time, took a last glance at the groups of dancers, and by mutual consent withdrew.

They walked arm in arm down the Avenue Friedland and the Boulevard Haussman, and separated at five o'clock in the morning on the Place de la Madeleine, after having agreed to meet at three o'clock in the afternoon, at the Hotel de Bade where Camille V— was stopping.

The officer awaited his friend at the appointed time, but he did not come. He was beginning to feel uneasy when a waiter knocked at the door and handed him a letter brought by a messenger which ran as follows:

"I attended that reception on the Avenue Friedland yesterday, in the hope that the noise and bustle might bring some diversion to my sadness. But it did not. For six weeks I have struggled in vain against the grief that absorbs me. Paris recalls too cruel souvenirs; I go, I know not where, straight before me; may your friendship forgive me for not saying adieu. I fear that you will interrogate me, that you may tear my secret from me, and I have not the courage to tell you now. But some day you will know it, my dear friend; when I have become more calm, more master of myself, I intend to write my curious and exceptional history. I will send it to you, and if you think it can be useful, I authorize you to publish it. You will not name me; I have full confidence in your delicacy, and no one will ever know who I am. What matters the rest! I do not even know what will become of me!"

Adrien de C— has kept his promise; we publish the manuscript received by Camille V— and which he has confided to us.

II

My start in life, my dear friend, seemed to indicate that I was born under a lucky star. I pursued my studies at the Lycee Bonaparte. I obtained many prizes at the annual examinations, and I carried off the grand prize for rhetoric. I presented myself at the Polytechnic school and passed third. Two years later I entered the school of bridges and dams, and left it with my diploma as engineer; I was at once intrusted with the construction of a tunnel on a new line of railway; it was a difficult task, innumerable obstacles presented themselves, but I triumphed over them to my credit and fame, and the minister made me knight of the Legion of Honor when I was barely twenty-five years of age.

Shortly afterward, I was offered a position to oversee important public works in Egypt; I accepted, and in ten years my fortune was made. I then returned to France, intending to enjoy my riches and create a more agreeable existence for myself, and perhaps to marry. It is here that my star began to wane. Hardly had I manifested my matrimonial inclinations, than my protectors, my friends, and especially their wives, proffered me a thousand offers of assistance. They vied with each other in their efforts to dispose of my hand. I was overwhelmed with invitations to dinners, balls and concerts. I was enticed to the country; I was presented to all the marriageable young girls in creation. These young ladies often deigned to smile on me, and their mammas encouraged them.

In fact, I was considered a good catch; young, knighted, rich and not bad-looking. I could choose from among the most charming and best-dowered. I had but to stoop and pick, as Mme. de F.—one of the most elegant of *Parisiennes* and my most zealous protectress, laughingly assured me.

Will you believe me, I hesitated to stoop; I was very difficult to please; I said: "this one is plain, that one is frightfully beautiful, that other suits me well enough, but her family is too large, I would look like the chief of a tribe; Mlle. A—dresses like a lady of the lake and Mlle. B— sings like a peacock." In short, I took pleasure in discovering faults; and I would have wearied the patience of M. de Foy himself.

Nevertheless, they brought new incentives; my hesitation and resistance exasperated my protectresses, but they vowed they would overcome my ill-dispositions. They no longer presented isolated heiresses, but a perfect swarm of them; I had but to choose from the lot. Before my

ADOLPHE BELOT

dazed eyes defiled pale and rosy faces; small, medium and tall figures; rounded and pointed shoulders; hair of every shade from jet black to light brown, from the ashen to the incandescent blonde; lips that were thin and lips that were thick, sensual and curling; noses of every shape and for all tastes. It was a never-ending procession, a perpetual magic lantern, a living kaleidoscope.

Ah, well! this defile wearied me—made me nervous. I finally came to look on the prettiest as plain, the most charming as insupportable, and instead of choosing from among those more or less divine creatures, I heaped maledictions on their heads.

"Ah! you are too hard to please," they said to me. "You can find one for yourself; we shall have nothing more to do with you."

"That is exactly what I ask! Hereafter when I enter your drawing-room, madame, you will not whisper: 'Look over there, to the left, on the third seat; she is pretty, is she not?—one-hundred and fifty thousand francs and expectations. And there, near the chimney-piece—that blonde, as witty as a demon, and a millionaire father. And that third, an angel; I saw her come into the world; I would answer for her as for my own daughter. And that other—, "But no, no, you tire me, madame; my head is not a weather-vane. I am merely a gentleman like the rest. I have the right to chat in a corner with a friend without having you telling me with your eyes: 'You are losing your time, young man; you are not here to amuse yourself, remember, but to see your future.' I can now abandon myself to the enjoyment of a game of ecarte; I am at liberty to relish an ice without being taken by the hand to be presented to an entire flock of emaciated young girls who have just invaded the drawing-room. Ah! I can now breathe, and if I ever take another fancy for marrying, I swear, madame, that I shall not warn you; you have spoiled me for the trade."

Three months glided by, three months during which I vowed in presence of all my friends that I would die a bachelor.

Ah! if I had only kept my word! But I must not anticipate.

On a beautiful night of the summer 186—I was sitting on a wire-seat in the Champs Elysees philosophically smoking my cigar, when three persons took possession of seats not two paces from me.

I glanced carelessly at my neighbors and at once saw that I was in the presence of an honest family composed of a father of respectable appearance, a mother of uncertain age and a daughter of twenty to twenty-two. Since their arrival they had been occupied watching the throng defiling before them and had not exchanged a word. The father now turned to the daughter and addressed her.

"Paule," said he, "I advise you to change your chair; it is damp."

"No, it is quite dry," replied Paule briefly.

"I assure you that you are wrong and you will cough this evening."

"Well, then let me cough."

"Now, my child, do be reasonable and do what I tell you. I speak for your own good."

Instead of answering, the young girl merely shrugged her shoulders. The father would, no doubt, have insisted again but his wife interposed.

"You are only wasting your time in trying to convince her," she said; "she will have her own way in spite of all you can say."

"Well!" thought I, "it seems this Paule is endowed with a pretty character. The man who marries her will be a happy mortal. And to think that she perhaps made part of that famous procession, that she may have been presented to me as a model of perfection. I must see if I can recognize her."

I drew my chair forward, for the tall figure of the father almost concealed the daughter.

I was perfectly dazzled, although I had seen some very pretty girls in those famous processions of a few months ago. But she surpassed the most beautiful!

Ah! my poor friend, never will I forget her, however I may reason, however I may struggle against my recollections, I evoke her vision in spite of myself and she immediately appears.

She advances, indolent and supple in her least movements.

Notwithstanding her youth she is charmingly developed, and her form, ample as a Spaniard's, displays more advantageously an elegant and slender waist. Her prettily arched foot, coquettishly encased in heeled boots, scarcely touches the ground. She approaches, and my whole being is thrilled. Mysterious and penetrating perfumes escape from her and intoxicate me. Before she speaks I already hear her voice, vibrating, accentuated, almost masculine. She bends toward me and I contemplate her.

What fascination in the large black eyes, half-veiled by long lashes and surrounded by a bluish circle! What beauty on the red and somewhat thick lips, slightly curled and covered with irritating down.

III

The reflections that I have just poured forth on the beauty of the young girl, whom chance had placed in my path, did not come to me then. I contented myself by thinking that my neighbor was remarkably beautiful, and I could not help being interested in her least movements. Futhermore, I must admit that she appeared quite unconscious of the attention she attracted; she did not once raise her eyes to me, and was not guilty of any of those innocent coquetries which even the most careful of young girls indulge in.

Her father and mother chatted together while she looked at the throng of promenaders, in a listless and dreamy way, appearing to take no interest in their conversation. Her dazzling beauty attracted the attention of every body; young or old they slackened their pace or turned back to look at her; she seemed completely indifferent to this admiration.

Once only did I see her start from her insensibility, to follow with her eyes a very pretty blonde who passed in front of her. The eccentric dress of this woman no doubt attracted her attention, and she turned to look after her.

"Evidently, Paule does not enjoy our company," said the father, annoyed by the obstinate silence of his daughter.

"I have already observed that," replied the mother sadly. "Paule cannot exist without Madame de Blangy; she is always lonesome when not near her, and we can no longer amuse or interest her."

This maternal remonstrance appeared to make a certain impression on my neighbor; she condescended to open her lips.

"It is only natural that I should take pleasure in the company of Madame de Blangy," she said; "we were schoolmates for six years, and she is still my dearest friend."

"We do not upbraid you for that friendship," replied the father, who seemed anxious to conciliate his daughter; "but we regret that it lessens your affection for us."

"You are mistaken, father," replied Mlle. Paule, "my affection for Madame de Blangy does not resemble the love I bear you, and can in no way interfere with it."

"I am glad to hear it. But come, chat with us a little while. Why did not your friend join us in our walk this evening?"

"She expected guests to dinner, but promised to try and find us later."

"I am afraid she will not find us; it is growing dark and the countess is a little nearsighted if I am not mistaken."

"Oh! do not fear; if she passes near I will recognize her," answered Paule.

This conversation, of which I did not lose a single word, for I had drawn nearer my neighbors, excited my curiosity all the more as the name of Madame de Blangy was well known to me.

I had met this lady several times the previous winter at Mme. de F—'s, my most enthusiastic match-maker, and had been struck by her beauty. I even believe that for several days Mme. de Blangy occupied my mind to the detriment of the marriageable young girls who defiled before me. As soon as she made her appearance I forgot all my engagements for the dance and all marriage projects, and went off to chat in a corner with the new-comer.

As fair as her friend Paule was dark. Berthe de Blangy possessed a particular charm; her large blue eyes reflected ingenuity and boldness, at the same time; her voice was of infinite sweetness; her exceptionally small mouth displayed charming teeth pressed closely against each other; and her round dimpled chin would have made an analyst dream. Even women could not help admiring her perfectly molded shoulders.

Her quick intelligence, prompt in retort, fertile in witticisms, astonished and charmed. Always armed with an eyeglass, she would suddenly stop in front of you, and with her grand, imperious air address the boldest questions, soon followed by a naive remark that would have made a school-girl blush.

In a word, she was a most charming woman, and for a short time I was so well charmed that one day I dared confess it. She came quite near me, brought her eyeglass to bear on me and said:

"You are wasting your time, my dear monsieur; I have had a husband, and that has sufficed to give me a horror of all men. I have no desire to replace him."

Instead of the words: "I have had a husband," she might have said: "I have a husband," for the Comte de Blangy is still living in some part of France, or in foreign lands. Rich, titled, highly respected by everybody, an attache of the bureau of Foreign Affairs, where his merits were much praised, he had two years before, at a reception in a drawing-room de la Chaussee d'Antin, suddenly found himself in the presence of Berthe and Paule, the two school-friends, the two inseparables, the brunette and the blonde, as they were called.

Struck by the beauty of the two young girls, he asked for information concerning them, was presented to their families, hesitated some time between the brunette and the blonde, decided in favor of the latter and married her. Six months glided by, during which M. de Blangy's friends remarked a great alteration in his features, a complete change in his character. He was sad, taciturn, avoided society and only made short visits to the minister's cabinet. He came for a last time in the winter of 186—to ask for an unlimited leave, pressed the hands of a few of his colleagues, and announced that he would travel for several years.

In fact, he left three days later, and no one ever knew whither he went.

Much comment was made in society on this sudden departure and complete disappearance, after six months only of marriage. A few tried to explain the count's conduct by pretending that he had been cruelly deceived in his marriage, and that he had simply left a woman who was unworthy of him, without recriminations, without outcry, like a true gentleman. But as this explanation rested on no proof, fact, or word from M. de Blangy's lips, the countess soon regained the popularity she had hitherto enjoyed.

Moreover, though her manners were eccentric, her conduct was beyond reproach. She received but few friends intimately and never went out except in the company of her friend Paule. Such was the woman awaited by my neighbors; and she did not delay in making her appearance among the promenaders.

I was the first to see her as she approached leaning on the arm of an old gentleman, whom she had no doubt requested to accompany her, and whom she dismissed as soon as she had rejoined her friends. She entered noisily into the group formed by my neighbors, kissed Paule on both cheeks, and sat down by her side at some distance from her parents.

I felt a great desire to hear a few words of the two young women's conversation, but they spoke so low that my curiosity remained unsatisfied.

Half an hour later they arose and went down the Champs Elysees, now almost deserted. The countess and Mlle. Paule walked arm in arm; the father and mother followed.

After their departure I arose in my turn, directed my steps to the *Cirque*, attended the last exercises and regained my bachelor apartments.

That night I slept badly. The remembrance of the beautiful Paule haunted me. Her features were already as deeply engraved in my mind as they are to-day. Her deep and vibrating voice resounded on my still charmed ears.

I saw her large eyes in turn bold and languishingly vile, and repeated to myself her least words.

Her animation in speaking of Madame de Blangy and the joyous light that had come into her eyes when the countess appeared, had impressed me particularly. A young girl who was capable of such friendship, must—I believe—be capable of loving in a ravishing manner. There must be in her heart, treasures of tenderness and love that would prove rare jewels in a wife.

The glimpse I had obtained of her character, far from giving me food for reflection, delighted me. All the young girls whom Mme. de F—had presented to me, were according to her, endowed with all the virtues imaginable, veritable angels that had strayed into this world; and by dint of perpetual contact with all these perfections I had come to long with all my heart and soul for some good physical or moral defect that would have changed me, but they never would furnish any. Madame de F—was determined to strip her proteges and place wings on their backs; and I was forced to yield. I was, therefore, enchanted to have found the dreamed-of imperfection myself in a young girl, who, no doubt, was marriageable; and I finally fell asleep at five o'clock in the morning saying to myself that if I had not sworn to be a bachelor, Mlle. Paule would suit me in many respects.

The next and the following days, I could not help thinking incessantly of my pretty neighbor; I even went to the Champs Elysees two or three times in the hope of meeting her again, but all in vain. At the same time, almost unwittingly, I gradually returned to my former ideas of marriage. I admitted that I never had any serious motives to abandon them. I found a thousand reasons to become disgusted with my bachelor life; my linen was badly washed; I was badly served, ill-fed; my valet robbed me; in a word, my house needed the intelligent supervision of a woman.

My long solitude began to weigh on me, and I acknowledged that the time had come to create for myself a home and a family.

After a week of struggle and hesitation, the agitation of my mind decided me to undertake a certain step indicated by circumstances. One fine day I presented myself to Madame de Blangy at her home, Rue Caumartin.

IV

The countess was alone in her drawing-room when I was announced, at about three in the afternoon.

"Well! you are not dead then!" were her words of welcome.

"Not quite, madame," I replied; "has any one told you so?"

"No, but as I no longer saw you, I imagined it."

"I believed you were in the country at this season, madame, that is why—"

"If you believed me in the country," she said interrupting me, "what made you think I had returned?"

"I had the pleasure of seeing you at the Champs Elysees, a few days ago."

"At the Champs Elysees! yes, it is true, I was there last week. Why did you not come and bow to me?"

"It was almost dark and you would not have recognized me, probably."

"Very likely, I have such poor sight!"

"Besides," I rejoined, "you were seated with persons to whom I am a stranger."

"Yes, the Giraud family, I remember; we are very intimate."

"So I understood from the impatience with which you were awaited—the young girl especially; she had been searching with her eyes through the throng for a long time, when you finally came."

Madame de Blangy took up her eyeglass, which hung around her neck, fixed it on me and replied:

"Paule Giraud is my intimate friend."

"You could not have chosen better," I replied; "Mlle. Giraud is deliciously pretty."

"Is she not?" said the countess quickly, as if pleased to hear her friend's praises; but suddenly changing her tone she exclaimed: "You love brunettes now?"

"Indeed, countess, I always loved all that is beautiful!"

"I congratulate you. But if I remember rightly, you were more exclusive last winter; you seemed to believe in blondes only."

"Do not reproach me; blondes will not believe in me."

"They must possess very badly constructed minds. Are you more fortunate with brunettes?"

"I have met but one who pleases me, and she does not even know me."

"That may be to your advantage," retorted Mme. de Blangy with habitual impertinence. "And that brunette is Mlle. Giraud, no doubt?"

"But, countess—"

"Come, do not try to mystify me. Have I not guessed the object of your visit? You remain six months without giving a sign of life, without leaving a card at my door; and all at once you drop into my drawing-room, unexpectedly, without a word of warning, to mention my friend's name in the very first words of our conversation, and to sing her praises. You must think me very stupid! There, you might as well admit the truth; you have seen Paule, you find her charming, and as you are attacked with the monomania of marriage, you have come to ask for information concerning my friend; am I not right?"

"It is true."

"I am glad to see that you are frank, at least. Well, then: Paule has just attained her twenty-second year; she is very pretty, as you know; intelligent, and I assure you very decided in her ideas—I tell you this because you would soon learn it without being told—and I must, moreover, inform you that her family can give her no dowry."

"This last detail has no weight with me."

"Really, you are frightful."

"I have worked until this day," I continued without noticing the interruption, "that I might marry the woman of my choice without taking her fortune into account. I shall only consider her qualities and the respectability of her family."

"Oh! as to Paule's qualities, she possesses some that are charming in my eyes," said Mme. de Blangy, with an almost mocking smile. "However, they might not be appreciated by her husband."

"Why not, madame?"

"Oh! men are so odd! But let us continue. The respectability of the Giraud family is well established. Madame Giraud is an excellent woman, kind, indulgent, incapable of believing in evil, and of an exaggerated weakness with her daughter. M. Giraud, chief-clerk in a large business house, leaves home every morning at nine o'clock, returns at six for dinner, and spends his evenings at the club when not obliged to return to his office. At the end of each month, he regularly brings two-thirds of his earnings to the ladies for household expenses and troubles himself about nothing else. He is a very honest man who sees no further than the end of his nose."

"There is then something to see?" I asked.

"I did not say that; I simply repeated a vulgar, but much-used phrase, which to my way of thinking describes M. Giraud's character very well. Now you know all the family; do you want other information? Ask; I am in good humor to-day; the weather is cloudy; my nerves do not trouble me; I am disposed to be friendly; I will do you almost a favor, and there I shall do so under the form of good advice."

"I shall be grateful."

"Return at once to Madame de F—where I met you last year, and say: 'Madame, you must now have a new assortment of marriageable young girls; be kind enough to parade them before me once more, and I swear to make a choice this time.'"

"In other words, my dear countess," I observed, "you advise me to think no more of Mademoiselle Paule."

"I simply advise you to return to Madame de F—"

"Because Mademoiselle Giraud does not make part of her assortment."

"As you will; I have given you my advice; will you follow it?"

"I must first know if it is entirely disinterested."

"Monsieur, you—"

"Yes, in the advice you have just given me, with a benevolence for which I am grateful, is there not a little egotism?"

"What do you mean by that?" cried Mme. de Blangy, quickly.

"Mon Dieu! countess," I replied; "the sentiment which I have dared impute to you is quite natural. We always regret the marriage of an intimate friend; she cannot belong to us as in the past; we often lose the influence we possessed over her, and sometimes even lose her heart."

"Oh! I do not doubt Paule; she will continue to love me."

"She would have reason to do so, madame," I rejoined; "and that is in her favor."

"Then," she said, "all that I have been saying to you for an hour, far from inducing you to relinquish your project, has only fortified it."

"I admit that—" I stammered.

"I am a good-natured woman; contrary to my habits, I gave you some excellent advice, and instead of following it, you seek for the interested motives that may have dictated it."

"But—"

"You have made me nervous, monsieur; it is only right that I should vent my ill-humor on you. And now will you allow me to look at you? Thanks to my near-sightedness, I believe that I know you but little. You used to pay me some attentions, but I must admit, though it is perhaps not very flattering for you to hear, that I took very little interest in you. But now, as it is a question of my friend's happiness, I have no longer the right to be indifferent."

And without awaiting my consent, the countess fixed her eyeglass, leaned toward me and scrutinized my face.

"The features are delicate, distingue," she said after a moment; "you are what is usually called a good-looking fellow."

While I laughingly bowed my thanks, she went on:

"Having rendered sufficient justice to your physical perfections, I must add that you are one of those men born to be loved, wisely and calmly, by a good little wife, but who can never inspire a veritable, passion. Women never become violently enamored of any men but those of notorious ugliness, or of accentuated and energetic beauty. Mirabeau and Danton are the preferred types. You resemble neither the one nor the other, and you can only aspire to moderate affections. On that score you are the husband for my friend Paule."

"What do you mean by that?"

"You may interpret it as you please."

"You no doubt mean to say," I insisted, "that it is not necessary for husband and wife to love each other blindly."

"I mean to say nothing. But let us resume the examination: now for the moral. Will you promise to answer me frankly? Remember that it concerns my friend's happiness and your own."

"I promise to say the truth and nothing but the truth."

"Were you a good student—at college?"

"Excellent; I always carried off all the prizes in my class."

"You were then a great worker?"

"I admit it, madame."

"And after you left college, you, no doubt, led a gay life in Paris?"

"I did not have time, madame, as I at once entered the polytechnic school."

"Very well; but when you left there?"

"I went to the school of bridges and dams."

"Better and better. And afterward?"

"I spent two years in the province constructing a tunnel."

"Very good. And when the tunnel was completed?"

"I left for Egypt, where I spent ten years digging canals and surveying new railways."

"Then your existence has been that of an anchorite?"

"Very nearly so, madame."

"You need not blush. Anchorites have their good side."

The mocking smile which had lingered over her lips for a few minutes disappeared; and she resumed in a serious tone:

"From the examination of conscience, to which I have subjected you, my dear monsieur, and to which you have submitted with good grace, I draw the following conclusions, as my legal adviser would say: You are a good young man, a true gentleman, and you deserve to be happy. I repeat once more, and this time from the bottom of my heart, return to Madame de F—; repeat to her the little speech we spoke of, and marry, as soon as possible, the plumpest of her proteges. But if you will not heed my advice, and persist in the project that has brought you here, I wash my hands of the entire affair. And yet it is probable that I shall advise Paule to marry you; for as she is destined to marry some day or other, you are after all the husband best suited for her. This is all I have to say. Au revoir and good-luck; your destiny is in your own hands."

V

S uch was my conversation with Mme. de Blangy. I have tried to retain all the shadings; I have reported all the details. Unhappily, they did not strike me then as they have since. I did not then attach to these good counsels—given in a moment of magnanimity for which I should have been thankful—the importance they really possessed; I persisted in believing her interested, and saying to myself that the countess, jealous of Mlle. Giraud's affections, wished in her egotism to delay her friend's marriage as long as possible.

Nevertheless, I would, no doubt, have renounced my projects and forgotten my pretty neighbors of the Champs Elysees, if chance had not thrown me in her path once more.

One evening, about a week after my visit to the countess, I saw Mademoiselle Giraud in a box at the opera, accompanied by her mother and a gentleman of about fifty years of age, whom I recognized as an old friend of my family.

The incomparable beauty of the countess' friend appeared to me this time under a new aspect; the lights gave her complexion a marvelous brilliancy; her large black eyes seemed to sparkle; between her red lips appeared teeth of dazzling whiteness, and her demi-decollete bodice gave evidence of superb shoulders. Seated in a corner of the orchestra, lulled by the music of Lucia, I never removed my eyes from all these perfections.

That evening decided my fate.

Between ourselves, my dear friend, I must admit that I merited somewhat the name of anchorite conferred on me by Madame de Blangy. My existence, from eighteen to twenty-five years of age, had been so busy that I had found no time to enjoy Parisian life, and in Egypt, as you know, opportunities are scarce.

I therefore longed to taste those joys, to live after having vegetated, to experience violent emotions; and Mademoiselle Giraud seemed adapted to procure them for me.

But, you have already understood, I was and am yet what is called unsophisticated. One cannot with impunity obtain the first prizes at examinations, the prize of honor in rhetoric, and come out third from the Polytechnic School.

Such successes must be paid for sooner or later. The intellectual faculties, when overstrained sometimes, choke down imagination, and it requires some of the latter to meet certain misfortunes, and to foresee all the perils. In a word, be as virtuous as you wish, but be aware of all human defects, that you may have them always before your eyes and be prepared for them. Have self-respect, but do not fear to give your imagination full scope when it is a question of others. I had not given sufficient attention to these excellent precepts, and Mme. de Blangy evidently understood me thoroughly when in dismissing me she said: "After all, you are the husband best suited for Paule."

I have already told you that an old friend of my family accompanied Mlle. Giraud and her mother at the opera that evening.

I hastened to join him in the foyer, during one of the entr'acts, to speak of her who was already beginning to have such great empire over me.

Unfortunately for me he never wearied of praising Mlle. Giraud, whom he had seen grow up under his eyes. She was charming, adorable. Happy the man who should marry her; she would make an accomplished wife!

I am fully persuaded that M. d'Arnoux—such was the name of this enthusiast—believed in good faith all he said. Furthermore, he was only the echo of public opinion. Thanks to our mode of living, we are obliged to judge young girls entirely from appearances, and they are usually favorable. One person only—and even that is doubtful—can give an accurate account; it is their intimate friend. I had been fortunate enough to know Mlle. Giraud's intimate friend; she had been kind enough to give me excellent advice, and I did not follow it. I merited my fate.

M. d'Arnoux was not long in perceiving the interest I took in his conversation. Guessing the cause he interrogated me on my projects for the future, and as he perhaps felt as much affection for me as for Mlle. Paule, he proposed to present me to her family. I was imprudent enough to accept. "I will judge for myself," I thought; "I will know which is right: M. d'Arnoux, a respectable old gentleman, or Mme. de Blangy, a giddy woman. If Mlle. Giraud gives evidence of possessing any faults that might endanger my happiness, it will be time enough to renounce my project."

What absurd reasoning; the enamored man, as I was beginning to be, never sees faults; if perchance they glare before his eyes, he palliates them, or if that is impossible, he—makes virtues of them.

Three days after our meeting at the opera, I made my first visit to the Giraud family, in their apartments on the same street as Mme. de Blangy's home.

I will pass in silence the details of that first visit and those that followed. M. Giraud received me with great cordiality from the very first day. His frank and open manner seemed to say: "Before receiving you into my house, I made inquiries about you with excellent result. I am delighted that you should think of my daughter. Win her, and I shall be overjoyed to sanction your union. At first Madame Giraud was more reserved. Perhaps she did not share the hopes her husband built on me; or else, being in continual intercourse with Paule, she had suffered from her character, and feared she might make a bad impression on my mind.

Little by little, however, when she saw that I was becoming more seriously enamored of her daughter day by day, and that Paule's faults did not seem to frighten me, the ice melted, and the excellent woman took a veritable affection for me.

As to Paule, I can never accuse her of having been coquettish toward me and to have enticed me into marriage. From the very first visit she displayed an indifference from which she never departed during the whole time of my courtship. But without appearing too innocent, I might have been mistaken regarding the nature of the sentiment that I inspired. What we take for coldness in a young girl is very often only reserve and timidity. We rejoice over what might frighten us, and the least presumptuous of men promises himself that after marriage, he will assume the role of Pygmalion, and his wife will be his Galatea. Such a role could not be otherwise than charming with the person I have endeavored to portray, and everything seemed to indicate that a breath would suffice to animate this admirable statue.

In short, six weeks after my presentation into the Giraud family, M. d'Arnoux undertook to officially ask the hand of Mlle. Paule for me.

The father did not attempt to conceal his joy; the mother embraced me with tears in her eyes; and when the daughter was consulted, she replied that she would do whatever her family desired.

As for Madame de Blangy, whom I had met almost every day in the Giraud home, but who had never made any allusion to our long conversation, she took advantage of a moment when we were alone the night of the betrothal to observe:

"Decidedly, my dear monsieur, you are an imbecile."

Far from being angry at this impertinent outburst, I laughed heartily, for I interpreted the words of the countess thus: "I am destined to see you marry my friend; she will no longer be mine, and I shall not know what to do with my time and affection."

Being accepted officially, I had now only to await the few days necessary for legal formalities.

Do you appreciate my situation, my dear friend? I do not pretend that it was sad, and I do not ask your sympathy for my fate; but, as a faithful historian I must relate all my little tribulations.

The days that precede a marriage are calculated to bring the nervous system to a veritable state of irritation. There are so many things to think of.

A friend awakens you to pay his compliments of—condolence; a former lover sends you four pages of epigrams, affecting to confound your marriage with your funeral, and proposes, though not invited, to assist at the sad ceremony. All the cities of France tender their services to provide the wedding gift; a cashmere merchant comes to your house to offer his exotic products. The ladies of the *Halle* bring you bunches of flowers, and the director of a bureau for nurses—yes, dear friend, a bureau for nurses—had the impudence to write begging me to remember him when the time came.

Then one must hurry the purveyor who has not yet delivered the furniture for the nuptial chamber, make indispensable visits, order the daily bouquets, the necessary carriages, go to the tailor's, to the mayor's office, beg Monsieur le Cure to be good enough to celebrate mass himself and ask him to deliver one of those little discourses which prove to the guest that you enjoy a certain consideration among the clergy of your parish. And lastly, one must think of confession; and this is quite an undertaking, I assure you, when one is not accustomed to it.

In fact, when a man is really in love with his fiancee, and sees the day so impatiently awaited approaching, his blood circulates more rapidly, his heart beats faster, and he cannot help feeling a little feverish shudder now and then. And when the great day comes, it brings neither peace nor tranquillity. After a sleepless night, spent in thinking of an infinity of things, he arises at dawn, thoroughly exasperated at being obliged to get into full dress at an hour when elegant Paris is still in bed, grumbles at the coachman for being late, hastens to his mother-in-law who believes herself obliged to be tearful, then his father-in-law takes him by the collar to utter in an impressive tone: "Make her happy."

We reach the church where the guests have been awaiting impatiently for an hour, become entangled with a funeral coming out of the middle aisle; at the altar we make blunder after blunder, sit down when we should stand, and arise when it is time to sit, respond yes for no, and *vice versa;* drop the nuptial ring, while the friend we have invited as best-man is cursing heartily under his breath. After the celebration, three hundred persons precipitate themselves into the sacristy, which is barely large enough to contain the dozen persons that compose the clergy of the parish. We are pushed, squeezed, pressed; the blood rushes to the face, and we feel that we are frightful, when we might have had such a good occasion to display our good looks. Finally we emerge from this crush to be assailed by a throng of beggars who shower blessings on us at fifty centimes apiece.

The day is terminated by some little family fete from which it is impossible to escape unless you are wise enough to run away with your wife, on leaving the church. But these abductions, which have become fashionable of late, are not always practicable. A thousand reasons may oppose it. The evening is therefore passed in the midst of a new family, coming from four points of the compass of Paris, and sometimes of France, to do you honor. You must smile on everyone, bear a shower of compliments, press all hands, and kiss all kinds of wrinkled faces.

You belong to everbody except your wife. At last the hour for retiring strikes; you forget the tribulations, the annoyances, you have just experienced, the fatigue that overwhelms you, for happiness awaits you in your new home; you fly there, rush toward the nuptial chamber—alas! for me mine remained obstinately closed.

VI

A h, well," I hear you say, "after a day so well occupied, you are not to be pitied; it gives you time to collect your thoughts. You are both young; you are married for life and you can easily make up for the night of which you are deprived. Go, without further recrimination, and sleep elsewhere; it is the wisest thing you can do."

It is easy to talk; sleep elsewhere, did you say? And where, I pray? Do you imagine that in my new apartments I had many disposable rooms and beds? No, my dear friend. After mature reflection on the question, and the attentive reading of the theory of beds in the "Physiology of Marriage," I had come to share the ideas of Balzac entirely. I had even, so to say, impregnated myself with many thoughts of the great Doctor of Conjugal Arts and Sciences, as he entitles himself. Allow me to cite those that are still present in my mind:

"The nuptial bed is a means of defense for the husband.

"It is there only that he can judge whether his wife's love is increasing or decreasing. It is the conjugal barometer.

"There does not exist in Europe, a hundred husbands in each nation who possess the science of marriage—or of life, if you will—well enough to permit them to occupy a separate apartment from their wives."

I shared the opinion given so clearly by one of the greatest writers of our epoch, and the only couch in my new apartments being occupied by Paule, I resigned myself to sleep on the sofa in the drawing-room, without removing my clothes.

It will not surprise you, my dear friend, if I declare that, notwithstanding the fatigues of the day, I slept badly. To begin with, I arose several times—if one can call it rising—hoping that my wife had relented and withdrawn the bolt. Vain hope—useless trouble. The door remained hermetically closed. After each fruitless attempt I again stretched myself out on the sofa, but sleep would not come. Without exaggerating the situation, I could not help searching the motive of my dear Paule's conduct, which, to say the least, was original.

"The bolt may be badly placed," I said to myself, "and may have slipped when the door was pushed." But no; when I knocked there was no answer.

"She may have been fatigued or ill and desired to be alone for the first night. She must have but little confidence in me; I would have understood at the least hint, and withdrawn, simply begging her for the loan of a mattress. She has three, while I—"

By this you will judge of my commentaries during that long night, and I will pass the rest in silence.

About eight o'clock in the morning, I heard the servants bustling about the house; and I hastened to leave my couch, as it would not have been flattering to be discovered there *tete a tete* with myself. I went into the dressing-room and tried to make myself presentable.

A few moments later I rang for the chamber maid; affecting to come out of the nuptial chamber, I gave her a few orders in the name of her mistress.

Breakfast brought me into the presence of Mlle. Giraud (you will not be astonished if I still call her by her maiden name.) She advanced toward me without showing either coldness or affection, and extended her hand as she might have done to a comrade whom she was pleased to meet.

Her morning toilet was wonderfully becoming; never had I seen her more beautiful and charming. She seemed perfectly rested—which was not surprising.

Her conversation was witty and gay, as if determined to enliven the house she had just entered and bring laughter and joy into it. She certainly did not seem like a bride; she was so much at her ease, gently giving orders to the servants, making suggestions and already taking the reins of the house, without stiffness or haughtiness, but with a sovereign grace.

And I was truly charmed as I listened, looking at her in silence.

I had too much tact to make any allusion to the singular manner in which I had passed the night. I contented myself by saying with a smile:

"You were no doubt very tired last night, my dear Paule?"

"Yes, very tired," she replied, "but I slept admirably and feel quite refreshed."

These few words seemed to contain an explanation and a promise; they satisfied me fully and brought back my good humor.

About three o'clock in the afternoon Mme. de Blangy was announced. She entered impetuously, as was her habit, kissed Paule and extended her hand to me.

"As you see," she cried, "I cannot do without my friend; you must resign yourself to seeing me often."

"It is not difficult to resign myself to that," I replied bowing.

"Oh!" rejoined the comtesse, "notwithstanding your amiability, I create no illusion for myself. I shall inconvenience you a little sometimes, but I am determined to take no notice of it; and I come boldly the very first-day, defying all rules of etiquette, that you may accustom yourself as soon as possible to my unceremonious and impetuous visits."

"You will always be welcome, countess."

"So much the better. You are wise; it is always to a husband's interest to be indulgent to his wife's intimate friend. Is it not?"

"Let me not speak of the interest, madame, but only of the pleasure."

"That is very gallant; and you are growing in my estimation. Take care, or you will attain gigantic proportions. Apropos, are you jealous?"

"I do not know. That depends."

"Well, for instance: would you be jealous if Paule told me her little secrets as a wife as she told me her girlhood secrets?"

"I have not thought of the subject, countess."

"Well, then! here is an occasion to think of it. I am going with your wife into her room; we shall close the door, and I warn you that we shall speak of you the whole time. If you stand this first trial there must be good stuff in you."

"Very well, we shall see if I possess the stuff," I replied.

As if she only awaited this permission, Mme. de Blangy gaily encircled Paule's waist, and the two young women ran out laughing.

Far from being vexed with the comtesse for robbing me of Paule's company, I almost rejoiced over the *tete-a-tete*. A married woman can advise a young girl, and during my night of insomnia, I had asked myself more than once if Paule were not in the need of some information. Beside, I must admit my more prosaic reason: I was worn out with fatigue and delighted to find an opportunity of closing my eyes for a few instants.

When an hour later I awakened, the two friends had returned to the drawing-room and were chatting near the fire-place. They were not aware that I was awakened; I examined them at my leisure.

The contrast they presented was truly charming; they set off and completed each other's beauty, as it were. Beside the blonde hair and blue eyes of Mme. de Blangy, Paule's black hair and eyes seemed more dazzling; the slight *embonpoint* of the former made the figure of the latter appear more slender and delicate. And together, they possessed all the charms and attained the utmost perfection.

I believe, moreover, that they never appeared prettier than at that moment. Their faces beamed with happiness, and their complexion, animated no doubt by the flames from the hearth, seemed more brilliant than an hour before when they had left the drawing-room to exchange their confidences.

I moved, and Madame de Blangy turned, saying:

"Have you slept well?"

"Why—" I stammered confusedly.

"There, you may as well admit it; we are not at all angry; on the contrary, we have been able to chat at our ease," she rejoined, smiling and looking slyly at Paule. "Now I will leave you alone together; I do not wish you to detest me. So au revoir!"

In the evening, no one came to disturb my *tete-a-tete* with Paule, who was as charming as she had been at breakfast. She conversed on a thousand subjects, discussed many questions with an intelligence and wisdom, often even with a depth that caused me veritable astonishment.

I believed I had married a young girl whom I should have to form, and I find myself in the presence of a developed woman who was witty, sarcastic, prompt in retort, with a shade of philosophy and perhaps of science in her imagination.

"But my dear, where did you learn all that?" I asked.

"I have learned nothing," she replied smiling. "I guessed it all."

"You must have a wonderful imagination."

"Oh! yes, too much for my own happiness, and perhaps for yours also."

"Imagination when well directed is not a misfortune."

"Yes, but it must be well directed," she said with a sigh.

"Why did you not unveil your delicious qualities to me before to-day?" I rejoined.

"Because I am not a coquette. I tried to dissuade you from marrying me, and would not display my talents. You would not listen to me; you have faced the danger; the wrong is irremediable and I now unveil myself—as you express it—that I may be agreeable at least—intellectually."

I did not then remark this last word which was pronounced very subtlely and with intention. In fact, all this conversation should have given me food for reflection; but how reflect at ten o'clock at night, the day following my marriage, and near a beautiful woman like Paule!

Soon I even ceased to listen to what she said; I only thought of looking at her and admiring her, and then suddenly losing my head, I clasped her in my arms.

She gently and calmly disengaged herself, smiling her sweetest smile, rang for her maid and left the drawing-room.

A quarter of an hour later I saw the maid coming out, and I directed my steps, in my turn, toward the happy door, the threshold of which I had not crossed the previous night.

Sure of being expected, I did not even knock, but simply turned the knob.

The door did not open. As on the previous night the bolt had been pushed. I knocked; no answer came. I knocked again more impatiently; same result. I spoke, called, pleaded; all in vain. Can you imagine me, my dear friend, asking as a favor to be permitted to enter my own chamber? For it was mine; I had no other, and independently of my love, it was only just that I should aspire to repose in a real bed. My nerves were in such a state of agitation that I was on the point of emerging from my own character, usually so calm and peaceable, and knock on the door with such violence that she would perforce yield and open it. The fear of ridicule withheld me; I had no wish to admit the servants to the confidence of my conjugal misfortunes. I silently pushed with all my weight against the door, in the hope that it would yield to my strength. Vain hope! I did not even hear the slightest cracking. The construction of the door was excellent, and I could only too well congratulate myself on that fact. What more can I add? This second night passed as agreeably as the first; with the only difference that as I was worn out with fatigue, I succeeded in sleeping more or less.

On awakening I found myself calmer than I could have hoped, less discontented with my wife and more disposed to excuse her. After reflecting as coolly as possible on our conversation of the previous day, and notwithstanding certain details that had struck me, I came to the conclusion that Paule, far from being an *ingenue* ignorant of her duties, had on the contrary very positive ideas on marriage; she thought, no doubt, that a husband should take the trouble of winning his wife and that meanwhile he should be delicate enough to appear to forget his rights. In the interest of our love, she wanted to make herself desired, and to belong to me as a sweetheart before becoming my wife. In a word, she considered it unjust and illogical to exact that on a fixed day, on leaving the mayor's office, a young girl should throw herself into the arms of a man whom she scarcely knows; and she had resolved to evade this barbarous custom.

These are the reasonings with which I tried to explain Paule's conduct; only I thought she might have given me a glimpse of her views. I should then have arranged our apartments differently and purchased a second bed in view of my prolonged celibacy. It was also possible that she was not quite aware of the way in which I passed my nights, and it was prudent to give her a slight idea of that drawing-room sofa, so narrow and hard, which had for two nights been my nuptial, or anti-nuptial couch.

"The sight will touch her," I said to myself, "and will probably inspire her with the good thought of abridging my term of probation."

After breakfast, which again reunited us and where we displayed a charming humor as on the previous day, I offered her my arm and proposed a little walk through our domains. She accepted with the best grace in the world, and we passed into the dressing-room where I did my best to make her remark that it contained nothing but chairs.

"This furniture is sufficient for the present," she replied simply, like a good houskeeper and an economical wife.

Leaving the dressing-room, we entered a small summer boudoir attached to the drawing-room. There I designated one of those circular divans, with silk wadded backs, which are placed in the middle of a room, and on which may be seated several persons, turning their backs to each other.

"It is very pretty and fashionable," I remarked, "but gather an uncomfortable place to sleep."

"Yes," she replied with a knowing smile, "one would have to curl himself around the back of it and that would be tiresome."

We then entered the study which I had reserved for myself and resumed the conversation where we had left off.

"It would be impossible to even curl up in this room," I observed; "I have neither divan nor sofa."

"Why not?" she asked.

"Because I expected to be rarely in my study; I took particular care in furnishing the rooms we should inhabit together."

"You were wrong," she said; "a married man's study should be comfortable and elegant. Tradesmen and even many friends are received in this room, which serves to give them an idea of the rest of the apartments. I would advise you to purchase one of those pieces of furniture, which I have seen in many places; in the day-time they form a divan and at night a most complete bed."

I looked at her; her eyes did not even shrink from my gaze.

"I will follow your advice, my dear Paule," I replied. "I shall go out at once and purchase the piece of furniture you mention; but as you see that I had nothing to replace it, where do you think I slept during the last two nights?"

"I thought," she replied without being at all disturbed by my abrupt question, "that you slept in this room; only I believed it more intelligently furnished."

This phrase irritated me, and I replied angrily:

"You then intend to continue to lock yourself in every night?"

"Oh! instead of questioning my intentions, it might be more amiable to guess them," she replied sweetly as she replaced her hand on my arm to return to the drawing-room.

The last phrase fortified my suppositions of the morning. I was not dealing with an *ingenue* or a school-girl, but with a wonderfully well-informed young woman.

Where had she acquired this experience, this science of life, this coquetry which consisted in leaving me in suspense? Could her mother have said to her: "If you wish to preserve your husband's love, you must make yourself appear distant. The greatest enemy to love in marriage, is the facility of relations; in view of her happiness, a married woman is permitted to conduct herself in her household as an intelligent mistress."

No, Paule's mother was too good, too simple a woman to give such advice; she must have taken marriage to the letter and fulfilled its duties without arguments or reasonings. It could be no other than Madame de Blangy, who, wishing to give Paule the benefit of her own experience of marriage, had traced her this line of conduct. Ah, well! my dear friend, will you believe it, this influence exercised over my wife, did not irritate me at the time; my esteem for the comtesse—an esteem shared by everybody—sheltered me from fear, and that *naivete* which you know is in me, did not permit me to admit that a well-bred and intelligent woman like Mme. de Blangy, could have any interest in tarnishing the purity of a young girl by pernicious advice.

Then, must I admit it, that knowledge of life which I had discovered in Paule, that resistance she opposed to me, attracted instead of terrifying me. Innocence, as you know, usually possesses a charm for none but old or corrupted men. Men like myself, who have not yet lived, are more easily seduced by the intrigues of skilful coquetry; they are not frightened in discovering in a woman a little knowledge of the world, and if they think of marriage, you often find them disposed to marry a widow.

Therefore, I often congratulated myself in seeing in Paule the incontestable advantages of a young girl combined with a certain precocious experience due to intelligent advice, or to a particular intuition of life.

The novel position of aspirant to my wife's affections possessed an original charm and developed my imagination which, I must admit, had been slumbering until then. I believe that if my choice had fallen on an ordinary young girl, I would, in accordance with my calm temperament and a certain kind of apathy, peculiar to my character, have subsided into a most prosaic and commonplace husband. With Paule, on the contrary, my whole being awakened, and by degrees I came out of that lethargy caused by the excessive activity to which I had abandoned myself in my youth. My intelligence having always been overtaxed and my mind incessantly distended over abstract studies, I had almost forgotten that I possessed a heart; it now beat for the first time, and I was delighted to feel its beating.

At last I would live and realize that charming dream—to be in love with my wife, unite fancy to reason, and replace by a good and beautiful passion, a love which, if Paule had acted otherwise, would have degenerated into a tranquil and insipid habit.

You will, therefore, not be astonished to see that I cheerfully transformed my study into a bed-room. I arranged it as comfortably as possible to endure the penance imposed upon me. Nevertheless, I was determined to employ all the seductions with which nature had endowed me to abridge my time of trial.

VII

Two weeks glided by, during which I was truly remarkable for my patience, discretion, and delicacy. I exacted nothing, I asked nothing, I did not even address a direct prayer. To see me so reserved and platonic in my relations with Paul, one might have thought that we were still publishing our bans and that we had not yet presented ourselves before the mayor or clergy of our parish.

I was courting my wife in the most assiduous manner, but I never made any allusion to the hopes which, you must admit, my dear friend. I had the right to conceive. Her reserve, however, equaled my own, and if I made it a duty to ask nothing, I must say that she showed no haste in promising anything. I was, therefore, no further advanced. Indeed it sometimes seemed to me that I was going backward; but as I lay in my bachelor bed one morning I consoled myself with the thought that if discretion did not succeed, it would perhaps be still time to pursue another system.

If, perchance, my dear friend, you are astonished to see my patience so soon wearied, I pray you to put yourself in my place for an instant. Do not fear, I would not leave you there very long, you have never harmed me and I have no wrongs to avenge on you. Imagine yourself beside an adorable woman, charming in every sense, desirable beyond all expression, to be in continual contact with her the whole day, to be charmed by her, intoxicated, infatuated, and when night comes—you know the rest. Now, what do you think of it?

The situation is not new, you will say; everybody has found himself in somewhat analogous circumstances; it often happens that a man courts a woman for weeks, sometimes months, without obtaining from her, for some reason or other, any encouragement. I agree with you. But the woman you courted thus was not your wife; many motives may have induced her to delay yielding her affection; on the brink of the abyss, a thousand fears, a thousand terrors, scruples of all kinds may have retained her; if her resistance and hesitations were a torture for you, at least you admitted and were even disposed to understand them.

But in this case, where, I pray you, do you see good reasons to explain such a prolonged resistance? Where are the fears, the terrors, the scruples? Lastly, where is the abyss?

I do not know why I try to convince you; I am certain you rallied in my cause before hearing me, and if I astonish you, it is by my unalterable patience, which you perhaps already call weakness and stupidity.

Ah, well! from the sixteenth day of my probation I lost all patience. Under the pressure of continual irritation my temper had sharpened, and I, who had long imagined I had no nerves, was now struggling against a multitude of nervous attacks.

This state could not last; since she seemed determined to repulse me, I resolved to formulate my plans.

"Already!" she said smiling.

Ah! in my present dispositions, I believe I could almost have strangled her for that word 'Already'! Did this woman understand nothing? had she no heart, no feelings? I believed I had married an animated being and I was united to a statue.

I suppressed my anger and tried to move her. I painted with eloquence the love she had kindled in my heart; I told her of my moral sufferings, of the physical illness which had taken possession of me, and of which she was the cause; I begged her to have compassion on me, for I had reached the limit of my strength.

She listened attentively and seemed affected by what she heard; but when I begged her to reply, she remained silent.

Ah! my dear friend, there are silences which cause atrocious sufferings!

"Speak," I cried, "speak; say what you will, but speak, I implore you!"

"I have nothing to say," she replied.

"Explain your resistance, your hesitation. I promise to find your reasons good, but give me one, one only, in pity!"

She made no reply.

Then, in a fury, I abruptly left the sofa where I had been sitting at her side and went in search of my hat to go out. I was so exasperated by her obstinate silence, my whole nervous system was in such a state of irritation, that I feared I might commit some violence if I remained near her.

Yes, a sharp word is so quickly uttered, an abrupt movement so easily escapes you, and women are so adroit in taking advantage of these outbursts. They never admit that they are the cause of them, that they have driven you to extremities, or that they were in the wrong. They quickly forget the sharp words that have wounded you, or their calculating reticence and the thousand needles they have driven into your heart; they only remember the last words that escaped from your lips, the significant gestures that you have made, and they transform these into terrible weapons against you.

"You are brutal!" they cry. "All is ended between us!"

You can easily understand that I had no wish to expose myself to be told by my wife that 'All is ended,' when nothing was commenced, and I hurried away in the fear of being unable to contain myself any longer.

But when I had taken a few steps toward the door, I suddenly turned back.

"Listen," I said, "you will not answer my questions. Very well! let us say no more about them. I ask but one thing; tell me at what moment will cease the trial you have imposed on me, and I swear on my honor to await that moment, however distant it may be, without complaint. But fix a date; do not leave me thus in suspense; the uncertainty in which I live exasperates me, kills me! Have pity on me, I have done you no harm; I love you, I desire you ardently! Is this a wrong in your eyes? Is it a crime for which I must be punished? There, be kind; let my prayers, my tears, yes, my tears, melt you. Look, I weep; it is stronger than myself; I suffer so much!"

Then, perhaps on the point of being moved, she gently pushed back the hands that tried to clasp her, and, rising, she rooted me to the spot by a glance in which I thought I read a menace that made me tremble, and passed into her room.

The same instant I heard the well-known noise of the bolt pushed into its place.

Here you interrupt me, do you not my dear friend, to cry: "But unhappy man, why do you not remove the bolt that stands in your way? Are you not in your own house?"

Reassure yourself; the idea that comes to you also occurred to me. I had more than once thought of asserting my authority. Since prayers, solicitations and tears were of no avail, I felt that they could only injure me in Paule's estimation. Women do not usually love men who beg and humiliate themselves. Supplications touch them only when they agree with their secret desires. They may perhaps give themselves through kindness of heart, but they never love through charity.

Mendicity is interdicted in the department of love.

It was time to take an energetic resolution, under pain of forfeiting Paule's good opinion.

One evening after dinner, she proposed that I should accompany her to Mme. de Blangy's house, as she had not seen her for two days. I assented, but when we reached the countess' door I made a pretext of a sudden headache that compelled me to remain in the open air, and left my wife there, promising to return for her.

Scarcely had I left her when I rushed back into my apartments; entering Paule's chamber, I loosened, one by one, all the screws that held the odious bolt in place, with the aid of an instrument I had purchased during the day. I broke the point of each of these screws and replaced the heads in the original holes, giving the bolt a fictitious appearance of solidity.

Paule would not perceive my stratagem; the bolt was still solid enough to be pushed into place from within, but the heads of the screws, being no longer held by the points, would fall at the least pressure on the door from without.

When I rejoined my wife an hour later, I found her in the countess' boudoir, half-stretched on a divan beside her friend.

Although expected, I thought my arrival seemed to disturb them. I have since thought that they were exchanging confidences; Paule's eyes were wet and fatigued as if she had been weeping, and I remarked more animation in the features of the countess.

On our way home, and in our drawing-room, before taking, leave of my wife, I renewed my prayers. I would have been so happy not to be forced to have recourse to extreme measures, and to leave her in ignorance of the little job of locksmithing I had done!

She was colder, haughtier, more discouraging than ever.

Had she spoken to me one kind word, given me one affectionate glance, made a tacit promise, however far in the future, I should certainly have renounced my design.

Nothing; not a word, not a gesture, not a glance. She seemed to not even hear me, not to even suspect my existence; I had never seen her so dreamy, so far removed from me.

I hesitated no longer. I said good-night and she withdrew to her bed-room. I waited an hour that she might have time to undress and go to sleep. Then, trembling, feverish, pale as a criminal, I directed my steps toward the door of her chamber.

As I expected, the bolt yielded and the door noiselessly opened.

VIII

I entered.

Imagine my amazement when I saw my wife seated in front of the fire-place reading, dressed as she had been an hour previous.

She turned nonchalantly as, I entered and said with the greatest calmness: "I expected you."

By a great effort I succeeded in controlling my emotion, and leaning my back against the chimney I faced Paule and said in my turn:

"Why did you expect me?"

"Because the bolt, in falling at my feet when I pushed it, revealed your project. It was you, was it not, who spent your time in doing this little job, which is worthy of a burglar or a lover?"

"Or of a husband," I added, "although they are rarely obliged to have recourse to such measures. Yes, it was I."

"You admit it."

"I admit it," I replied in a firm tone. "My present lore is ridiculous and I am resolved to play it no longer."

"What did you hope, if I had not discovered your stratagem?"

"I hoped to prove my love for you."

"In doing me violence," she said with a disdainful smile.

"Yes, in doing you violence if you drove me to it; but heaven is my witness, that before resorting to this extremity I did all in my power to move you. Neither my patience, my delicacy nor my prayers have softened you."

"Believe me, I am less moved just now than ever."

"You cannot be less, since you have never been moved."

"You know nothing about it. In any case, your conduct of this evening has filled me with indignation, and I warn you it is useless to return; all your attempts will henceforth be in vain."

"Ah! it is my conduct of this evening that dictates this determination?"

"Yes."

"It is false!" I cried vehemently; "for until to-day you have had no occasion to reproach me. I have overwhelmed you with cares and attentions, and you took no pity on me! What reason have you to act with such severity? I must know."

She remained silent.

Then, in a paroxysm of nervous agitation impossible to describe, I seized her by the wrists, clutching them with such force that I compelled her to arise.

"Answer; I must know!" I repeated.

"You hurt me," she cried.

"Answer, you must answer me!"

"Well, then! No, I will not answer! Never will violence get the better of me. Ah! you do not know me yet. Well then! learn to know me; it will serve you for the future. What I want I do want; and what I do not want will never be accomplished. Your strength will wear out against my will and you will exhaust yourself in useless struggles."

Though she spoke with such harshness, and though each word struck me to the heart, can you believe it my friend, I could not help gazing at her and admiring her.

Her long hair had become loosened and fell in waves over her shoulders, her breast heaved, her eyes shone with a flame I had never seen, and between her deeply colored lips, more sensual than ever, appeared her charming teeth clinched angrily together.

"Ah! how beautiful you are!" I cried.

And forgetting all that she had said to me, I caught both her hands in my left and holding them tightly, tried with my right to approach her head to my lips.

She struggled with such energy and displayed such strength to evade my embrace that she soon escaped from my arms, and I fell back, crushed, on the chair she had previously occupied.

Then, taunting me with my defeat, she folded her arms saying:

"Do you still think you could get the better of me by violence?"

"Then you hate me!" I cried wildly with tears in my eyes.

As in most nervous crises, emotion succeeded anger.

This strange young girl, touched perhaps by my suffering, moved no doubt like myself by the struggle she had just made, took up a cushion, approached my chair, seated herself beside me and said:

"No, I do not hate you."

I looked at her; her eyes no longer had their habitual expression; they were tender and kind.

"Then if you do not hate me, why do you torture me?" I asked.

"Do not question me on that subject," she said gently; "I assure you that I cannot answer. But I swear to you, that far from hating you I feel a veritable affection for you and appreciate all your qualities. I am deeply sensible of all your attentions, and to be frank, I admit that I already forgive you for your stratagem of this evening, and for your anger of a little while ago. I am too intelligent, believe me, not to understand and excuse them."

"Why have you never spoken and reasoned with me with this gentleness?" I asked.

"Because I feared you would misunderstand the nature of the sentiment you inspire in me, and encourage a love to which I could not respond."

"These last words, my dear Paule, do not agree with what you said a few minutes ago. If you appreciate my qualities and if you feel a veritable affection for me, I can hope—"

"No, no," she said quickly interrupting me, "you can hope nothing, and that is why I hesitated in opening my heart to you. I feared the reasonings you are now making."

"Admit that they are logical."

"Very logical, I admit; otherwise I would not have feared them."

"I do not understand you."

She again resorted to silence.

"Come," I rejoined, wishing to take advantage of her softened mood, "trust to my affection. I do not speak as a husband but as a friend who will be very indulgent to you. You have perhaps in your heart one of those young girl loves, of cousins let us say for instance, to which you attach an exaggerated importance. Well! far from making it a grievance, I will treat you as a sick child; I will surround you with affection and await your recovery."

"No, it is not that," she replied.

"Then I will continue to seek, and—"

"You will not find," she concluded, "and it is better that you should not find. Say to yourself: 'It is thus,' and try to make the best of it."

"That is impossible, my dear friend; I am your husband legally at least, if not in fact."

"The marriage was not of my seeking," she retorted. "You contracted it toward and against me. Recall the past; you saw me for the first time one evening at the Champs-Elysees; did I turn my head once in your direction; can you reproach me with the shadow of coquetry? No. You then hastened to Mme. de Blangy; you spoke of me and of your projects; what did she answer: 'Paule is not a suitable wife for you; renounce her!' Notwithstanding this, you were presented to me; you pleased my father and mother; could I then close the door of a house of which I was not mistress? I displayed a coldness toward you which I did not feel; for I repeat it, you pleased me from the first. Three weeks went by, and you did not fear to propose for my hand. My whole family tried to persuade me that you were suitable to me in every respect, and I was convinced of it myself. I resisted, however, and as I had already rejected three offers of marriage without giving a single motive for my refusal, my father became angry and threatened the convent. The convent! Imagine me at twenty entering a convent when I have no religious inclinations! I became alarmed and ended by saying to him: 'Let your will be done!' But to you I said: 'Renounce your projects; I cannot refuse you, but you can withdraw your proposal. You deserve to be happy, and I cannot contribute to your happiness.' Instead of heeding the advice, you attached no importance to my words. You persisted in taking me for a child who knew nothing of life; with that presumption peculiar to all men, you were sure of winning my love and you married me. There! I leave it to yourself; is it my fault? and can you reproach me for what has befallen you?"

"Then," I said after a moment's silence, "because I have loved you enough to be deaf to all warning, I am condemned perpetually to the most frightful of tortures; that of Tantalus."

She took my hand, which I had not the courage to withdraw, and went on:

"The torture will not be as painful as you imagine; I will assuage it by my devotion and affection. If I do not love you as you desire, at least, I will never love anyone else; I swear it, for you are the only man who could have pleased me. You will never have cause to reproach me with coquetry toward yourself or the friends to whom you may present me. If you desire it, my life shall be spent with my mother, yourself and Madame de Blangy only. I will surround you with so much affection and attention that the world will believe you the happiest and most beloved of husbands. In a word, I shall be the best of sisters to you."

I reflected in silence for a long time on all she had said. I tried to consider calmly the situation she offered and to reconcile myself to it. But suddenly my blood boiled, my flesh revolted, and rising from my seat I cried passionately:

"No! I do not accept the bargain you propose. I love you with passion, with delirium, and I cannot consent to live at your side as a brother. I married you that you might be my wife, and you must be that!"

"Ah!" she retorted, "I have been told that all men are egotists and brutes. You are no better than the rest. Well! I repeat it, you may accept or not accept what I have proposed, but I will be none the more yours for that reason. I have said all I had to say, and I pray you to leave me now; I am worn out; I need rest, and if you have the pretension of being a husband, I imagine at least, that you have no wish to be a tyrant."

IX

E ven in this she was mistaken. I did become a tyrant.
What had I to spare? Had she left me any hope? Could I
believe that in time I should triumph over her resistance and succeed
in touching her heart? No; she had explained herself clearly on the
subject and it would have been madness to form new illusions. I was
condemned, without possibility of hope, to perpetual celibacy.

I exercised my tyranny, however, without conviction, without any
clearly defined plan, with days of rest and abrupt returns to kindness
and affability. It was an intermittent tyranny.

Ah! my dear friend, do not reproach my weakness, my want of
energy; it is difficult to be continually harsh to one we adore!

My first act of authority was to occupy myself with the bolt question.
"Useless pains," you will say, "the little job of locksmithing you performed
during the day did not profit you much! It is not the door of your wife's
chamber you should unbolt, it is her heart." You are perfectly right. But
being unable to triumph over moral resistances, I tried to overcome
the material obstacles. I would allow no barricades in my own house,
and, I proposed to enter, whenever I pleased, the only bedroom of my
apartments. I therefore carefully picked up the little instrument of
my torture from the carpet and placed it in my pocket.

Strangely enough, the same day, although no workman had entered
the house, I found a new bolt, stronger than the first, fixed to the door.
Who had placed it there? My wife evidently. Without a word, I armed
myself with my screw-driver and undid what had been done. The next
day a new bolt appeared. It suffered the fate of the two others. I began
to have a collection. My wife did not yield until the seventh bolt; she
had no doubt exhausted the stock of the neighboring ironmonger.

These little operations fortunately took place between ourselves, far
from the eyes of the servants. They continued to believe us the happiest
couple in the world, so much did Paule overwhelm me with attentions
in their presence. Never by a word or gesture could they have guessed our
internal quarrels. I am pleased to render this homage to Mademoiselle
Giraud; it is the only one.

Did she use stratagem to replace the seventh bolt? Did she find
an original way of fortifying herself and escaping from my ill-timed
nocturnal visits? For a long time I remained in ignorance. The

remembrance of my first campaign made me reflect; I hesitated to expose myself to a new defeat, and I shut myself up like the hunter, who after many unsuccessful attempts, remains in his tent through the fear of being laughed at.

However, this access of timidity, of vanity, of dignity, of cowardice—call it what you will, I believe there was a little of each—could not last.

The thought came to me—it would have come to anybody else in my place, that I should not resign myself to my sad fate without waging a few decisive battles. On the night of my defeat, I had fought an enemy on her guard. The bolt in falling to the floor, had announced my near arrival, as a detonation on the ramparts announces a near attack to the besieged. Paule had immediately armed herself from head to foot; she had ranged her batteries, and as soon as I had the imprudence to appear, she had opened fire on me and I had fallen crushed and bruised under the assault. This time, I would surprise the enemy in the night, during slumber, when she would be without arms and without munitions of war.

I had determined to show neither pity nor mercy; to be moved by neither prayers, cries, nor threats; to be resolute and energetic, whatever happened; and to gain one of those victories, so dazzling that the conqueror is absolved of the ruses of war which he has employed.

It was not without a certain emotion that I saw the approach of the hour fixed for the great battle; I knew that it would be decisive. When two adversaries, equally armed, meet at close quarters in broad daylight, the vanquished does not feel humiliated; he can send a new challenge the next day, which must be accepted. But if we make a night attack on a surprised and disarmed enemy, we must conquer or forever renounce the impossible struggle.

I, therefore, neglected nothing that might assure a brilliant triumph; I chose my time, my hour, and I even went so far as to try to guess the tactics that my adversary would employ to resist me, the manner of defense she would resort to, and the ruses she would oppose to mine.

On that night, my wife retired to her chamber at about eleven o'clock; I followed her example and retired to my study. I waited a long time, until all noise in the house had ceased, all lights had been extinguished, then, at about one o'clock in the morning, I softly traversed the drawing-room and entered the nuptial chamber without encountering the least obstacle. The door closed noiselessly behind me.

A lamp suspended from the ceiling threw a soft and mysterious light around me. I looked toward the bed.

Paule was sleeping. Her face was turned toward me, one bare arm was gracefully curved and reposed on the pillow above her head. Under the sheet that covered her but imperfectly, I could see the outlines of an admirable form. I saw all this at a glance; standing in the middle of the room in my gallant deshabille, exposed to the danger of taking cold, the time was ill-chosen to gaze upon my wife as she lay voluptuously stretched in my domain. Was it not my duty to reconquer it as soon as possible and to install myself there as master before the awakening of the usurper?

I decided to make the assault. This was no easy matter however; the bed was one of those good high ones such as our fathers loved, and into which it is difficult to climb. It was a high step—there was no denying it. But my resolution was taken, and I knew no obstacles. Suddenly, at the very moment when my right foot had already crossed the edge and was seeking a point of repose on the elastic summit, when my left foot was about to rejoin it, at the moment in fact when I was, as I might say, suspended in the air, I was startled by a peal of laughter—a peal of laughter that resounded so loudly that I lost my equilibrium and fell back on the carpet.

Paule had not made the least movement; her arm was still curved above her head, her limbs gracefully crossed, but her wide-open eyes were fixed on me and she was laughing—laughing!

Then with one bound I landed on the foot of the bed. Can you imagine me, my dear friend, in that posture and the costume you may suppose, tall as I am, with my face half hidden by the curtains. You find me very ridiculous, do you not? And to think that I still had to cross the distance between the foot and the head of the bed.

I undertook the voyage.

Paule was still laughing. Finally I bent down, raised the coverings, brought them over me and stretched myself my whole length. Ah! what a bed! how large it was; I had taken my place in it without disturbing Paule. How soft it was, how well I had chosen it! Paule was not laughing now; she was looking at me. I was looking at her also, without daring to budge from my place. Was I not master of the situation, was not victory assured?

Alas! no. It was not. I was prepared for everything, except the obstinate silence of my wife and her freezing impassibility. I had expected

ADOLPHE BELOT

to encounter an adversary who would complain, insult me, fight; I was ready for the combat and I would have come out victorious. But those two large eyes that looked at me with a stubborn fixedness, those obstinately closed lips, that inert, insensible, almost inanimate body, froze me in my turn. My fine resolutions vanished.

Oh! she well knew what she was doing. Some one had indicated her this line of conduct. Some one had said to her:

"The more loving a man is, the easier it is to impress him; the more his nerves are stretched, the more easily they relax at the first nervous commotion. A too vivid emotion can transform an athlete into an infant. He forbids you to bolt the door; obey. Let him penetrate into your chamber which he will not abandon to you, sleep on your two pillows; he is not to be dreaded, you have nothing to fear from him. He will understand the futility of his clandestine visits, he will blush over his defeat and will not again expose himself to the acting of so ridiculous a role."

She who dared give her such advice was right. She knew to perfection the defects of our poor human nature, its weaknesses and discouragements.

From that time I dared not penetrate into my wife's chamber, and, strange to say, I no longer dared complain; was not her door open to me; had she expressed surprise at my ill-timed visit? No. I could only reproach her with the coldness of her welcome; but I should have conquered that coldness, and I had not. I was truly in despair. I had now no more hopes or resources. I had already asked myself more than once if I ought not to confide my troubles to Mme. Giraud, if it were not permitted me to say: "In giving me your daughter, madame, you had no wish that we should live separately, but we do. Use your influence with her to make her understand that marriage is not merely a sinecure."

But what would have been the result? Mme. Giraud would have scolded her daughter, who would have answered—if she had condescended to answer, which is doubtful—

"My husband is a calumniator, if through a feeling of exaggerated modesty I have sometimes closed my door, I do not do so longer. Nothing prevents him from entering, and he does enter. If he does not find himself comfortable there, it is his own fault, not mine, and it is I who should complain of him."

The conversation would end there, as Mme. Giraud would have nothing to reply. One person only, in consequence of her subtleness, her experience of life, the originality of her character, and the real influence she exercised over Paule, could address to her a few observations and make her understand that the wrong was not all on my side; that it was in some sort the consequence of her own actions. But I hesitated in mixing Mme. de Blangy in our household affairs, in taking her as the confidante of our domestic troubles. I dreaded her peculiar wit, her mocking humor, the darts she would not fail to level at me, and even her way of examining me at short range.

X

I was mistaken, however; Mme. de Blangy, whom I finally decided to take as confidante, showed herself a really good woman. She made me relate my misfortunes in the most complete manner, allowing me to omit none of the details. Far from being wearied by my tale of woe, she seemed to take pleasure in listening, to take comfort in it, as it were, and when I had terminated she said kindly:

"I was somewhat prejudiced against you, but now you have all my sympathy."

I gave these words a simple significance.

"Being my wife's intimate friend," I said to myself, "Madame de Blangy may have feared that Paule would transfer all the affection she had for her to me. My confidences have reassured her; she now sees very clearly that I am not loved; that Paule does not deceive her when she assures her that she still loves her; her jealousy has disappeared and she esteems me."

She gave me the proof of this by assisting me in trying to discover the motive that might have alienated my wife's affections. But we could discover none.

We also sought a means of drawing me out of my false position; notwithstanding all her tact Mme. de Blangy could think of nothing. However, seeing me so desolate, so crushed, she took pity on me, and ended by saying:

"I am going to Havre for a few days to visit a member of my family; if you will confide your wife to me, I will occupy that time in tutoring her, in trying to instill better sentiments into her heart, in teaching her to love you."

I accepted gratefully, and hurried back to Paule to tell her to prepare at once. The idea of this journey seemed to delight her; she immediately went to her friend to fix the day of departure.

They left the next day and I accompanied them to the station of the Rue Amsterdam.

"I am quite hopeful," whispered Mme. de Blangy as she pressed my hand in leaving. "I will bring her back an entirely different being."

But the journey brought no change to my situation. From a certain alteration in Paule's features, however, I had reason to believe that Mme. de Blangy had kept her promise; that she had scolded and tormented her on my account. But it was written that nothing should triumph over this indomitable character.

It was then, my dear friend, that, irritated, vexed, enervated, I became wicked and gave free scope to the tyranny of which I have already spoken. As long as I had some hope, I controlled myself, notwithstanding my nervous paroxysms and real grief. I did not wish to be accused of any wrong, and if not as attentive as a loving and beloved husband, Paule could not complain of me. I left her free to dispose of her time according to her own fancy, to see the persons that pleased her; I procured a sufficient number of distractions, and I had more than once brought her gifts destined to soften her. But now I refused to accompany her when she went out; whenever she wished to attend a concert or an opera, I gave business as a pretext to remain at home. I no longer escorted her into society, and closed my doors to visitors. I even cut down the household expenses. In fact, I knew not what to imagine! I had vainly tried to win her by kindness; I now tried to conquer her by famine. However, I must do her the justice to say that she never complained of my proceedings; she never uttered a reproach or an observation. She seemed to make it a duty to be as submissive in some things as she was obstinate in others. She was no doubt conscious of her wrongs toward me, and pretended to expiate them by the evenness of her temper and the charms of her gay and lively intelligence. Even jealousy had no effect on her implacable serenity. Yes, jealousy! for, in my despair I tried to make Paule jealous. It was folly, you will say, and I am entirely of your opinion. I who when a bachelor had never had anything more serious than secret and passing liaisons— if they can be called liaisons—now that I was married, took a mistress openly. I suffered that a renowned actress whom all Paris knew, should advertise me; I even asked her to do so as a favor. I left her open letters lying about in our apartments, and dispatched the answers by one of our own servants.

One day at the table, I paid in Paule's presence, a bill of six thousand francs for ear-rings I had presented that morning to Mlle. X—. Finally, my dear friend, I slept out, yes, actually slept out.

You will perhaps think that my wife could not be aware of this. But I beg to tell you that I entered late in the morning, and made so much noise, that the whole household was aware of my immorality. In short, I was becoming cynical!

You may perhaps think that from the day I emancipated myself, Paule believed it her duty, for form's sake at least, to show her displeasure. On the contrary, she had never been more amiable, more zealous to please me. And the more she overwhelmed me with her indifference and tameness, the more exasperated I became, the more efforts I made to wound, move and draw her from her apathy. At last, I thought I had discovered a means of being disagreeable to her, and perhaps force her to ask for mercy; it was to separate her from her friend, Mme. de Blangy, with whom she spent all her afternoons, and nearly all her evenings since I neglected her.

One day as she was preparing to go out I stopped her.

"Where are you going?" I asked.

"I am going to see my mother as usual, and then Berthe."

"I think you visit Madame de Blangy a great deal too often."

"Why do you think so?" she asked, raising her head and looking at me.

"Because—" I stammered, trying to think of something to say. "Because her society does not suit you; she is too worldly a woman for you."

"Berthe! worldly! She scarcely receives any visitors, seldom makes calls or goes out in society."

"She evidently does not find herself at ease there; her position of discarded wife, of married woman—without a husband, places her in a delicate position."

"It is well known that the wrongs are all on her husband's side."

"Not at all; many persons doubt it; myself, for example. Experience has demonstrated to me, that in certain households the first wrongs come from the wife. I have reflected deeply on the subject; Madame de Blangy's society might compromise a woman as young as you—a young girl almost."

"It has taken you a long time to find it out!" she observed without seeming to notice my allusions.

"I should probably never have found it out had I not been so cruelly disappointed in you."

She allowed this last thrust to pass unnoticed also.

"I thought the countess was your friend," she rejoined.

"She is too much your friend to be mine!"

"That does not prevent you from asking her services!" she retorted.

"She does not render them."

"That is not her fault."

"So much the worse. A woman of her age, experience and position should have more influence over you."

"Oh! she has a great deal."

"She exercises it badly, then; and for that reason she is the more dangerous."

I had evidently succeeded in moving Paule; for the first time she was roused from her indifference. Therefore, at each retort my courage increased. Had I at last found the sensitive chord? Her friendship for Mme. de Blangy, her fear of losing her, would no doubt decide her to capitulate.

"What conclusion am I to draw from all you have said?" she asked after a short silence.

"Oh!" I replied determined to strike a decisive blow, "the most simple conclusion; you shall see the countess no more."

"Not at all?"

"Not at all!"

"And if I wish to continue to see her?" she cried, aroused from her ordinary calm.

"I shall prevent you," I replied.

"In what way?"

"First, I shall forbid my servants to admit Madame de Blangy, and they will obey me."

"I do not doubt it. But if I cannot see her here, I can see her in her own home."

"No, you cannot."

"Do you intend to lock me in."

"Not at all."

"Then?"

"I shall simply go to the countess and say: Madame, I beg you to cease all relations with my wife."

"And if she refuse?"

"She cannot refuse. Her peculiar position obliges her to exercise extreme circumspection. She is fully aware that she would be ruined in public opinion if it were known that in spite of the expressed wishes of a husband she continued to attract his wife to her home. In good society, there exist certain laws and customs which we cannot evade under pain of being ostracized."

Paule undoubtedly understood the justice of my arguments; she remained thoughtful.

ADOLPHE BELOT

"May I at least pay a last visit to Madame de Blangy," she asked after a moment's silence, "to tell her of your wishes and express my regrets in being deprived of her friendship?"

"Certainly," I replied, touched in spite of myself by her submission.

When she had gone, I admitted to myself that this submission must be only assumed. Paule had no doubt gone to hold a consultation with the comtesse to find some means of changing my determination. What did it matter? Was I not resolved to show no weakness, to be inexorable, as long as she was inexorable with me.

I was mistaken on that point. Paule never opened her lips concerning Mme. de Blangy; neither did the latter make an attempt to regain her friend; she did not even write, as I had expected, to abuse me for my conduct. I had no need to close my door against her, for she never came to it, and I had positive proof that Paule did not visit her. Did not Mme. de Blangy live in the same street, almost opposite to us, in fact, and when my wife went out, could I not, from my window, concealed behind the blind, follow her with my eyes, and convince myself that she passed the countess' house without entering?

"This cannot last!" I said to myself; "they are both too proud to ask me to allow them to renew their old existence. They count on time, on reflection, on my love, to soften me; but when they become forced to admit that they cannot count on that, then—"

Ah, how wretched I was! to so eagerly love a woman who did not care for me!

Never, perhaps, had my nerves been more unstrung than at this epoch. Never had my love been more ardent. My liaison with Mlle. X had no doubt brought about this result; when beside the woman you do not love, you are always tempted to think of the adored one. You see her, you hear her, and say:

"Oh! if it were she!" Your head swims, and she who was to cure you of a love for another only augments it.

XI

Time glided on, and Paule recovered all her placidity. She seemed to have forgotten Mme. de Blangy; and above all, she seemed to have forgotten that I was her husband. Nevertheless, I still hoped.

I counted on my tyranny, on the seclusion in which my wife lived, and the desire she must feel to see her best friend once more.

But I soon lost all hope. This is what happened:

One morning, while I was reading the newspapers in the drawing-room, Paule passed into her dressing-room. She came out of it some time afterward, her shoulders covered with a cloak, her hat on her head and said:

"I am going out shopping, and I shall also stop to see my mother. Have you any messages?"

"No, thank you," I replied.

"Au revoir, then," she added, and went out.

As soon as the door closed behind her, I ran to my usual post, at the observatory I had established, being the blinds of my study, which, alas! had also become my bachelor bed-room.

It was only to acquit my conscience that I still went to this trouble, for during two months Paule had always passed Mme. de Blangy's house, without stopping, without even raising her glance to her friend's window, and she had no reason to depart from her usual habit on that particular day. I soon saw her on the walk below me, following the houses in the direction of the boulevards. I surprised myself in admiring her; her hair reflected dazzlingly in the sunlight. Once in a while she raised the bottom of her dress, to avoid some obstacle, with an almost imperceptible gesture, and I could see two dainty little feet and two deliciously formed ankles.

She did not walk, but undulated, as it were, her shoulders, bust and hips seemed to roll from right to left and from left to right. How seductive she appeared!

Suddenly a wild idea flashed through my head: "If I follow her," I thought, "I will see her longer."

I swear, my dear friend, that at the moment I obeyed—at least I believe it—no sentiment of jealousy. I was charmed and desired to remain under the spell; that was all. I forgot that Paule was my wife; that was certainly easy enough to forget.

I rushed down from my apartments, sure to find her again as the Rue Caumartin is long, straight, and crossed by few streets. I had not gone twenty steps in the direction of the boulevard when I saw, at a short distance from me, on the same walk, the same little feet, delicious ankles, hair, shoulders, and back. All these continued to undulate; I followed the undulations.

When she reached the extremity of the Rue Caumartin, before crossing the Rue Basse du Rempart, Paule seemed to hesitate. Would she go in the direction of the Madeleine, or the Bastile. Suddenly, before deciding, and as if obeying a secret intuition, she turned and looked behind her. I had barely time to take refuge in a door-way; she did not see me.

Evidently reassured, she took the boulevard and walked toward the Madeleine. But her uncertain steps, her gestures, her glance behind her, her evident uneasiness, made me reflect.

"Can she fear being followed?" I asked myself. Was I becoming jealous? That would be the last straw!

You are perhaps astonished, my dear friend, that I had not been jealous before. But I had no reason to be. Since our marriage, Paule's existence had been most regular, and entirely devoid of incidents; she made but few visits, received rarely, and went out alone only to see her mother and her friend.

I could always account for the use of her time within a half-hour. Under those circumstances how could I suspect her of infidelity, or feel any jealousy? When I tried to guess the motive of her hesitation, the thought came to my mind that she might have a lover. But I was at once obliged to concede that this was impossible, unless she gave him rendezvous in our apartments, in her mother's or in Mme. de Blangy's house. The three suppositions were inadmissible.

When she reached the Place de la Madeleine, she directed herself toward the church, ascended the steps and entered.

"What can it mean?" I asked myself; "does she make her devotions on week days now, when she does not even think of going to mass on Sunday?" Then, another thought struck me: "Can it be her piety that is the cause of my troubles? Can she be accomplishing a penance which she makes me share? Can it be that we are both the victims of a vow pronounced in a moment of enthusiasm? Oh! then I may hope; one does not pronounce eternal vows; this one must be only temporary."

At the same instant I started and rushed in the direction of the Marche de la Madeleine. A new thought had struck me; Paule had simply entered the church to baffle any one who might be following her, and she would come out of a side door. Why did I precipitate myself to the right instead of to the left side? I do not know, but I soon had cause to congratulate myself on my choice. I had scarcely concealed myself behind one of those little structures used by flower-venders, when my wife reappeared. She had merely gone through the church as we cross a public place. And to think that a moment before I had suspected her of devotion! There could be no mistake; she was going to a rendezvous, and was merely taking a round-about way.

She resumed her walk, and I resumed mine, keeping about thirty paces behind her, on the qui vive, ready to vanish like a shadow the moment she turned her head. Jealousy had transformed me into an expert detective. She now took the boulevard and walked rapidly. At times I was seized with a wild terror; if that throng of promenaders should hide her from my sight, if I lost her! Then I would run and suddenly find myself two feet from her, behind some stout personage built to serve as a living wall. At the Boulevard des Italiens, I almost lost her. I thought I had seen her turn into the Rue de la Chaussee d'Antin, but a rapid glance to the right and left convinced me of my error. I returned to the boulevard and came up with her again as she was turning into the Rue du Helder.

My position was becoming perilous; the street which Paule now took is not much frequented; the walks are narrow, the gate-ways nearly always closed and the shops few. It was difficult to vanish abruptly, and the least imprudence would have betrayed me. But I committed none, thanks to the detective qualities so suddenly developed within me and which would certainly have been appreciated in the Rue de Jerusalem. Instead of following my wife at a few paces as I had done until then, I contented myself by following her with my eyes, and resumed my run only when she reached the Rue Taitbout. There I could again follow in her shadow without danger.

Where were we going? when would we stop? For a few moments certain indications led me to suppose that I was approaching the end of my peregrinations. Paule seemed more uneasy, her steps were less regular, she turned more frequently, not that she knew she was followed, but no doubt because the moment had come to redouble her precautions. Ah! my dear friend, what a run, what a pursuit, what a chase, and, above all, what emotions!

Finally she turned to the right, into the Rue de Provence, passed the Rue Saint Georges, crossed the Boulevard Lafayette, turned into the Rue Laffitte and suddenly disappeared through a gate-way.

I stopped. What should I do? Enter the house in my turn, overtake her on the stairway, reproach her for her conduct, treat her as she deserved, and oblige her to follow me?

But then my secret would escape me; she would refuse to admit that she had come to a rendezvous—explain her presence in this house by some simple pretext, saying she had been given the address of some trades-person whom she was seeking. She had entered the Madeleine to pray, she had turned at each instant merely through curiosity, and that it was only for the sake of lounging that she had promenaded through the whole of Paris before reaching the Rue Laffitte. Oh! she would not have been embarrassed I assure you. She would have succeeded in confounding me, perhaps even in convincing me, of her innocence. Would it be of any use to speak to the concierge? She must be known; this was certainly not the first time she entered this house. But the man might be devoted to her, refuse to answer me, and warn her! Then all would be lost; I would not obtain the proof of her perfidy, I would not learn the name of the man who dishonored me, I could avenge myself neither on her nor him!

Ah! avenge myself! what delight after so much suffering! In the interests of my vengeance I resolved to be calm, patient, and crafty. I resolved to wait. Wait! wait at this door, before the house where I was certain she deceived and betrayed me, where she accorded another what she refused me. What torture!

An empty carriage was passing, I beckoned to the coachman, directed him to stop at the corner of the Rues Laffitte and de la Victoire, then I entered it, closed the windows, fixed my eyes on the door-way through which Paule had disappeared and waited. Two hours went by. Two whole hours! At last she came out. A thick veil covered her face, one of those English woolen veils which are used by adventuresses. She stopped on the threshold, glanced around her, hesitated a moment, then suddenly taking her resolution she walked rapidly in the direction of the boulevards. I remained some time at my post of observation, hoping to see the one she had just left. No one appeared, or rather my suspicions could not rest on any of the persons I saw coming out. I alighted from the carriage, dismissed the coachman, and returned homeward. Paule was already installed in the drawing-room.

"How late you are?" she exclaimed as I entered.

I was on the point of exploding, but controlled myself.

"Have you been waiting long for me?" I asked.

"Yes, quite a while."

"Are you satisfied with your walk?"

"Perfectly satisfied. The weather was so beautiful I took advantage of it and made several calls."

"Did you see your mother?"

"No, she was out. If you permit me I will go this evening."

"Certainly."

At this moment dinner was announced; I offered my arm to Paule and we passed into the dining-room.

XII

Do not be astonished at my sang-froid and the control I managed to keep over myself, my dear friend. I was less to be pitied than you suppose. Yes, less to be pitied; I no longer groped along in darkness, I was no longer surrounded by mystery, I had no longer to search the motive of her coldness and indifference. I now held the key to the enigma I had so long vainly tried to solve; I no longer faced a sphinx but found myself in the presence of a woman, made like the rest, faithless as the most of them. In short, I could doubt no longer; Paule rejected my love because she had a lover.

Ah, it was indeed terrible and I suffered cruelly, but I knew the nature of my ill, at least, the name of my malady. I would certainly know the man who had reduced me to this despair, who had dared take possession of my property, of my rights, robbed me of the heart that belonged to me, to keep it for himself only without giving me the smallest share.

Ah! the wretch! he had no doubt said to her; "I consent to let you marry him, to let him give you his name, but it is I alone who shall be your husband. You will take no heed of his love and his rights. You will love but me."

Yes, he had said all this, and had torn a solemn oath from her; if he had not she would have acted like most married women who have a lover; she would have deceived me with him and deceived him with me. But who was he? I must see him as soon as possible, I must know him, I must—

Ah! my dear friend, if you knew how my imagination which had never before been awakened worked now, how delirious it was and what schemes of vengeance it conjured! I assure you that my comrades would no longer have ridiculed my pacific nature; I would have frightened them by my ferocity.

Alas! the next and the following day I had no occasion to exercise it. Paule did not go out. The day of rendezvous had probably not come. Their love was intermittent and meanwhile I was in despair. To be reduced to despair by the uniform good conduct of my wife! At last, on the third day after breakfast, she announced that she would take a walk.

"In what direction?" I asked.

"I don't know," she replied, "wherever my fancy will take me; to some shop, no doubt."

"Shall I accompany you?"

"I shall be delighted," she answered totally untroubled, "I shall put on my hat and rejoin you at once."

What adroitness in baffling my suspicions, what artfulness! Had I not known otherwise I might have thought that I disturbed her in none of her plans. I was forced to pretend a business engagement that she might go alone.

This time I was not imprudent enough to follow her. Did I not know where she was going? I took a carriage and directed the coachman to the place where I had stationed myself a few days previous. According to my calculations, I still had some time to spare before Paule could reach Rue Laffitte, for it required more than an hour to come by her habitual circuitous course. A number of idlers stood at the angle of the Rues Laffitte and de la Victoire awaiting a chance errand. I called the most intelligent looking of them to the carriage.

"Do you want to earn a louis?" I asked. He made a quick affirmative sign. "Well then," I continued, "you will remain near my carriage as if conversing with the coachman. When I touch your arm, you will look before you and see a lady entering that third house to the right. You will wait a few seconds, then follow her up the stair-way and return to tell me at what landing she stops. It is very simple as you see; only the person in question must not suspect that she is followed.

You must be careful not to stop at the same landing, and hold a paper in your hand as if you were doing an errand for some one in the house."

I had no need of repeating my instructions. My man understood. A quarter of an hour later Paule arrived; I gave the signal, the man interrupted his conversation with the coachman and a second after disappeared through the same door. In five minutes he returned to me.

"Well?" I said interrogatively.

"The lady stopped at the second floor," he replied.

"Which side?"

"At the little apartments that overlook the yard, at the right as you go up."

"She rang of course. Who admitted her?"

"She did not ring. As she ascended the stairs she took a small key from her purse and opened the door herself."

This last detail changed my suspicions into certainties.

"Very well!" I said giving him the louis; then to insure his discretion I added, "I will perhaps require your services again at the same price."

That day my wife shortened her visit, and consequently my watch. Really she was becoming delicate. As soon as she had disappeared I left the carriage and walked toward the house she had just left.

To enter into conversation with the concierge I had determined on a most vulgar ruse, but one that usually succeeds.

"You have apartments to let?" I asked of the woman who was seated in the lodge.

"Yes, monsieur, on the fourth floor. We have one on the second also."

"Ah! on the second, that would suit me better. In front or overlooking the yard?"

"On the front; the rent is five thousand francs."

"It is a small apartment then," I said carelessly. The woman who had remained seated while answering my questions, now arose. A person who was not satisfied with apartments of five thousand francs merited a certain amount of consideration.

"No doubt, monsieur, you would find larger and more beautiful apartments in the new quarters, but this one has four bed-chambers."

"Ah!" I replied, having matured my scheme, "I must have five."

"There is a small parlor that might be changed into a bed-room. Would monsieur like to see it?"

"Very well, I shall look at it."

As I had supposed from the report of the man, two doors opened on the second landing. A large folding-door opened into the apartments I was to visit and at the right was a smaller one with a brass lock. I followed the concierge and conscientiously examined every room.

"It is to be regretted," I said when I had finished my inspection, "the apartments suit me in many respects. They are perfectly situated and well ventilated. If it were not for my son I would not hesitate to engage them."

I dared give myself a son, I who had not even a wife.

"Would not monsieur's son like it?" she asked puzzled by my words.

"He would complain of not having his private entrance. My son is a young man and he consents to live with the family but on condition of enjoying his liberty. If, for instance, you had small apartments of two or three rooms on the same floor, it would do very well. Unfortunately, you have no small apartments in the house."

"You are mistaken, monsieur; we have apartments that vary from eight to twelve hundred on each floor. But we have none vacant at this moment."

"How annoying! The apartments opposite these would have suited me so well! I have long searched for something of the kind."

I played my role with so much conviction that as I had hoped the woman said:

"We might perhaps arrange matters. The proprietor is very anxious to rent these large apartments, and if it suits monsieur we could secure the smaller by giving notice to the present tenant."

"Oh! it would not be right to disturb any one who has been here for a long time to oblige a new-comer."

"Oh! no, monsieur, this person has been here but two months."

"Ah! two months! the tenant is now settled."

"Oh! not much. The occupant lives in the country, it seems, and took these apartments only as a resting place, passing a few hours merely when in Paris—that is, two or three times a week."

"A young man who lives with his family and gives his rendezvous here no doubt," I said smiling.

"No monsieur, the tenant is a lady."

A lady! I was amazed! My wife had then the audacity to rent these apartments herself to meet her lover. I could not even console myself with the thought that driven by passion she had consented to come to the home of the one who pleased her, that she had succumbed little by little, as many women succumb. No! she had prepared her own fall— she was its author; like Marguerite de Bourgogne she possessed her little Tour de Nesle.

"If monsieur desires," resumed the concierge, "I can see the proprietor to-morrow, and I am sure we can make some arrangements."

"That will do very well," I replied recovering my composure. "But I would like to visit the apartments you mentioned. I cannot rent them without seeing them."

"Oh! that is easily done. The lady has given me charge of her rooms and as I have a key, monsieur may enter."

"To-day?"

"Not to-day, it is impossible. Madame is in Paris; I saw her come up."

"Has she not gone?"

"I think not, monsieur."

Evidently this woman neglected her business. The tenant had gone an hour ago, and she did not know it. My wife had been fortunate in her choice. But as I could not insist I resigned myself.

"Could I visit the apartments to-morrow?" I asked.

"Certainly, monsieur, madame never comes to Paris two days in succession."

"I will come to-morrow then, and as I expect to become your tenant take this as earnest money." I wanted to make an ally of this woman.

XIII

I was punctual at the rendezvous; the next day at two o'clock I was in the Rue Laffitte. As soon as she saw me, the concierge—remembering her earnest money—greeted me with her most gracious smile, came out of her lodge and preceded me up the stair-way. When she reached the second story, she took a pretty little steel key from her pocket introduced it into the lock and stood aside to let me pass. How fast my heart beat, how I suffered in penetrating into this mysterious refuge! I would now see the surroundings that witnessed the pleasures I alone should have known. I would, as it were, touch her treachery and infamy with my finger. When I had traversed two rooms, I stopped and addressed the concierge.

"The apartments are not furnished," I observed.

"I have told monsieur that it is merely a resting place; madame never sleeps here. She always comes in the day time and remains in the parlor."

"Where is the parlor?"

"This is it." I pushed open the door and entered. At first I saw nothing. The blinds were closed and the curtains lowered. The concierge hastened to admit the sunlight and I looked around me. Imagine, my friend, a small room of about four meters square; a boudoir rather than a parlor, hung with black satin decorated with deep red satin buttons. One of those immense Turkish divans, very low, almost level with the floor, covered with stuff similar to the hangings, encircled the room; on the floor was a rich heavy carpet, and a few black satin cushions belonging to the divan were scattered here and there for seats. The only ornaments on the wall were small Venetian mirrors and Louis XV chandeliers supporting half-consumed rosy candles. In the middle of the chimney-piece was a reduction in marble of the Baigneuse of Falconnet with a group of Clodion on each side. An ebony etagere, inlaid in pearl, stood opposite the chimney supporting a crystal vase filled with Turkish cigarettes and a few books in red morocco of which I caught the titles. There was a volume of Balzac containing: *Une Passion dans le Desert*, and *La Fille aux Yeux d' or; Mademoiselle de Maupin* by Theophile Gautier; *Religieuse*, by Diderot, and *Mme. de Chalis*, Ernest Feydean's last novel.

This, my friend, is a faithful description of the asylum. The originality of the furniture and the oddness of certain details did not strike me until long afterward, when I was called upon to remember the past. Having visited the boudoir, I asked the concierge if there was not another room.

"Yes, there is a dressing-room," she replied.

Summing up my courage, I entered expecting to see some eccentric device. I was mistaken; the room was barely furnished. The windows were hung with chintz curtains and on the little marble table were a bowl of Bohemian crystal, a tortoise shell comb and a box of poudre de riz.

"This room is not large," observed the concierge, "but it is very convenient on account of its closets."

"Closets! let me see them."

I was no doubt on the point of penetrating some mystery by finding clothes that would give me some information in regard to my rival. But, notwithstanding my search in every corner under pretext of examining the depth of the closets, I discovered no trace of redingote, coat or even smoking jacket. Instead I found a sort of cloak in antique white cashmere, lined in deep red satin—the same shade I had remarked in the boudoir—and a long black satin dressing-gown lined in pearl-gray quilted satin.

Must I admit this new weakness? I could not detach my gaze from these clothes which evidently belonged to my wife and which were still impregnated with subtle perfumes. I imagined I saw in this dressing-gown her admirable form in all its voluptuous grace. The red satin of the cloak and the pearl-gray of the dressing-gown displayed charmingly the whiteness of the skin and cast vigorous shadows on the adorable body. My wondering imagination even went further; I saw Paule suddenly emerging from her cloak, as the Ingres Odalisque might emerge from its frame, and advancing, moved and agitated toward the one she had preferred to me. Ah! what would I not have given to be in that man's place! I believe that if some one had said to me at that moment: "You have discovered all, the guilty ones are confounded, forgive them, do not use the rights that the law gives you, and your wife will be your wife; for you she will don the cloak she wore for another, she will join in the boudoir so full of light and color; for a week, a day, an hour, her smiles, her kisses, her caressess will be yours; you will enjoy all the delights you have incessantly dreamed of since your marriage and which always evade you. Ah! what I am about to confess is unworthy, cowardly; but I would have forgiven! Everybody, I know, cannot understand me. Many would be tempted to say:

"You can no longer love that woman. In learning what you have just learned, in discovering her treachery, scorn must have killed your love."

However, the impression I had experienced during my visit in the Rue Laffitte, melted away a few hours later; I recovered possession of myself, and was the more animated by the sentiments that belong to an outraged husband, to a man cruelly struck in his honor.

Two long days glided by, two days during which Paule evinced no disposition to go out; her thoughts sufficed her no doubt, and aided her in awaiting the hour of her next rendezvous.

At last the hour struck; I saw her start off with a light and tranquil heart, a thousand leagues from supposing what was passing within me. The door had barely closed behind her when I descended in my turn. Ten minutes later I was in Rue Laffitte. I was going to follow the plan I had clearly traced out.

"I demanded forty-eight hours for reflection," I said to the concierge, "and to-day I am almost decided. A few details alone prevent me from definitely engaging your large apartments. I desire to place some old chests and ancient tapestries which I would not cut under any consideration; it is therefore important that I should see if they will suit the drawing-room. I have taken the exact measurements and if you will permit me, I will now measure the height of your walls."

To give more weight to my words I took a paper covered with figures from my pocket. The concierge found my demand only natural and hastened to open the apartments I was on the point of renting. As they were empty she had no fear to leave me alone with my calculations, and she returned to her lodge.

At last! I was free! In a few instants I would see Paule ascending the stairway and stop at the opposite door. Her lover was perhaps already awaiting her and might come out to meet her; then I would rush on him. Or perhaps he would join her later; in that case I would face him as he inserted the key in the lock; forbid him to enter and demand satisfaction.

A quarter of an hour later I heard footsteps on the stair-way. My door was ajar and I could see to perfection without being seen.

It was my wife. She ascended hurriedly like a person anxious to arrive, or one who feared being followed. When she crossed the landing, she passed so near me that I heard her quick breathing. Motionless, one hand on the door, the other pressed against my beating heart, I looked on. She produced a key from her pocket and opened the door.

No one came to meet her and no voice welcomed her. She had reached the rendezvous first evidently, the other would soon come or perhaps he was already there and did not hear her enter. This last supposition must have been the true one; three quarters of an hour went by, many persons ascended the stairs, but none stopped. It was not probable that he would make my wife wait so long. Then the cloak lined with red satin came to my mind. In spite of the three doors that separated me from Paule, I saw her enter the dressing-room, I saw her don this voluptuous garment, then rush back into the boudoir, curl herself on those soft cushions in front of the fire, where the ruddy reflections from the flame warmed and caressed her ravishing form; then I saw my rival advance, bend over her and clasp her ecstatically in his arms. Yes, I saw all this, and a wild rage came over me. I was rushing to break down the obstacles that separated me from them; I wanted to appear suddenly, surprise them in the midst of their transports, strike them, kill them! But reason whispered: "Be calm, be prudent, before you can reach them, break down all the doors, they will have time to place themselves on their guard, the noise will attract the neighbors, they will take you for a burglar or a madman, arrest you perhaps, and then he will escape you! Suffer a moment longer; he must come out at last, and then—you can avenge yourself!"

I waited. Another three-quarters of an hour went by. At last I heard a door open, then a second; a sound of voices struck my ear.

He was accompanying her. I would see him. The outside door opened slightly, my wife appeared, and while opening it to pass out I heard her say these words:

"Day after to-morrow, at the latest, I promise you, and I will try to remain longer."

Then I made a wild rush; with one hand I quickly pushed my wife aside while with the other I forced the door wide open and found myself face to face—

XIV

I magine my amazement when I found myself face to face with Mme. de Blangy! Bewildered, I stared at her without speaking.

She appeared utterly stupefied also. My violent entrance certainly sufficed to cause her agitation. She was the first, however, to recover her self-possession.

"Why it is your husband, my dear Paule," she said. "His arrival was so abrupt that you probably did not recognize him. There is now no reason why you should hurry off."

When Paule had closed the door, Mme. de Blangy turned to me and said in her natural voice:

"I am delighted, monsieur, to receive you in my humble dwelling; pray be good enough to follow me."

As I did not answer, she took Paule's arm and led the way. I followed them into the boudoir. There I recovered my speech. But alas! I might as well have been silent, for all I could find to say was this useless phrase:

"Then I am in your house, madame!"

"What, you ask if you are in my house!" she cried laughing. "Did you doubt it? In whose house did you suppose you were entering in that cavalier fashion? In your own perhaps. I admit that in that case your manner would be more natural. But no, you are really in my own house. You are probably astonished to find that I possess two domiciles. The explanation is very simple. In the Rue Caumartin, I am incessantly disturbed; there is always somebody pulling at my bell; I have not a moment of liberty. Here, I enjoy perfect tranquillity. I retire to this refuge as the wise men of old returned to the desert—to dream. In this boudoir, I enjoy all the advantages of the country—silence, isolation, calm, repose—and I have none of its inconveniences; the crowing of the cocks, the barking of the dogs and the smell of the stables. I arrange my life to please myself; here I am independent, I am a bachelor."

She had delivered herself of this all in one breath, without a rest, with the object, no doubt, of making me dizzy with her babbling and mastering the situation. She stopped at last to take breath and with wonderful tact she met the objections I might have made, the astonishment I might have expressed.

"I see," she resumed laughing, "that you are looking around you—in stupefaction, permit the expression. You are saying to yourself, that for a retreat this boudoir is very luxurious, its furnishings very eccentric. This large circular divan, these Venetian mirrors, the groups on the chimney, shock you a little, you must admit. My dear monsieur, if I place statuettes instead of a clock on my chimney, as is the custom, it is first because I detest customs, and then I love to forget the time here. This divan is a delicious piece of furniture, the model of which I discovered in the Turkish department of the Exposition Universelle. There, just recline on it a little and see how comfortable it is. As to the mirrors, you would have thought them marvels if you had made your little—irruption half an hour sooner. Then the candles were lighted, the fire was burning, and a thousand lights were reflected in all these little mirrors; it was divine But I intended to go out soon after Paule's departure, and as I was far from expecting you, I thought I might extinguish the fire, blow out the candles and allow the sun to penetrate. But the wretch produces no effect here—forgive him."

I did not need Mme. de Blangy's recommendation to forgive the sun; he was not the one against whom I was angry. But then against whom was I angry? I no longer knew. The countess had succeeded in bewildering me; my head was swimming. While she spoke of the chimney, the divan and the mirrors, I had alternately glanced toward the points and objects she designated. I now mechanically cast my eyes on the famous cloak I have described so minutely; it had been carelessly thrown on the divan near the place where Paule was sitting. It simply belonged to Mme. de Blangy, and to think that it had impressed me so deeply! I had caressed the satin rapturously; I had inhaled the perfumes that escaped from it in ecstasy; I had dreamed of it; such is imagination! One would have thought that the countess guessed all my thoughts.

"You admire my cloak," she said suddenly, "and you are right. It is a delicious garment to wear at home."

She arose, took the cloak and put it on her shoulders.

"See how becoming it is to me," she continued; "in spite of its ampleness it displays the bust and shoulders admirably; and the folds fall so gracefully! Paule is wild over this garment; you should order one like it for her. I would offer her this one, but unfortunately we are not of the same figure."

I nodded my head in approval without speaking.

"But are you dumb?" she cried. "Here I am employing all my arts of coquetry and you do not even deign to open your lips. What is the matter? Ah! I have it! How strange that I did not think of it before.

Monsieur is furious because we have disobeyed him, transgressed his orders; he has forbidden his wife to see me again and she sees me. He follows her and unfortunately acquires the proof of her disobedience."

She came and seated, or rather stretched, herself on the divan at my side.

"Come, let us reason a little," she continued. "I will begin by telling you that I bear you no grudge for what concerns me. You are jealous of your wife's affections, you demand that she love no one but you. This is somewhat presumptuous, but that is no reason to be offended. Two months ago, when Paule announced the measures you had taken in regard to me, the ostracism you had declared against me, I simply exclaimed: 'Poor fellow, how he loves you!' As you see I am a good princess, or countess, I should say. I would have been more annoyed, it is true, if I had feared that you would succeed in separating me from my best friend, if I had not found the means of obeying while disobeying you, in a word if I had not solved the difficulty. 'Then he refuses to receive me,' I said to Paule. 'Alas! yes,' she sighed. 'Ah! well it is his right, and I will not present myself at his door again. He also forbids you to visit me?' 'Yes,' murmured the poor child with another sigh. 'You must obey him, my dear, a husband's orders are sacred; you will not set foot in this house again; but he has not forbidden you the Rue Laffitte since he knows nothing of my little country house, my secret retreat. You will come there and spend an hour with me two or three times a week. We will close the blind, light the candle, recline on the divan, smoke Turkish cigarettes and say the most abominable things against your husband in revenge for his ferocity. It will be charming.' This is what we have dared do, my dear monsieur. If we are guilty, take one of those cushions and suffocate us Turkish fashion; it will accord with the local coloring. If you forgive us for loving each other and rebelling against a separation, leave off that ferocious air, which reminds me of Bluebeard, and accept this cigarette."

She continued to chatter thus for half an hour; and when we took leave of her neither Paule nor I had found an opportunity to utter one word. This did not prevent her from saying:

"You may come and see me again in my retreat as you do not disturb its tranquillity by the sound of your voices. I do not reproach you, but you are rather silent and discreet."

This reproach was the last straw.

Well, my dear friend, what do you think of it? Should I not have been in raptures? The suspicions that had tormented me for a week had flown as if by enchantment. My jealousy had no cause to exist. It was evident that Madame de Blangy spoke the truth; she had rented those apartments to live as a bachelor, as she assured me. And in point of eccentricity nothing astonished me on her part. She had furnished them in her own way, and now when I recalled a thousand details, I was surprised that I had not thought of her on the occasion of my first visit with the concierge. Had she not a similar piece of furniture, in black satin and deep-red silk, in her drawing-room of the Rue Caumartin? Had I not many times heard her bewail the fact that Turkish divans were not adopted by Parisian furnishers? And should not those books on the etagere have made me reflect, since I had already remarked the bindings in her own home! As the countess had observed, my wife was only guilty of having spiritually eluded my orders. I had no serious grievance—that is no new grievance—against her. Alas! I was still at the same point! And nevertheless, would you believe it, I was overwhelmed by a deep sadness, a melancholy more profound than ever. For a week my jealousy had diverted my grief; I had dreamed only of vengeance, duel and death. And now that the cause of this jealousy had suddenly ceased to exist, I was obliged to abandon all my warlike projects, I remained in *statu quo*. My terrible fixed idea returned, and I again found myself face to face with the enigma that tortured me without relief.

The worldly distractions I had tried to taste had not been successful. I had long since broken off with the creature I have mentioned; those relations filled me with disgust; the remedy was worse than the disease.

The idea came to me that I should travel. "Movement, bustle, the sight of new horizons, the necessity of occupying my mind with a thousand details, of speaking of indifferent things, of living a life of activity, will make me forget," I said to myself. "At any rate, if I cannot master my thoughts, if I carry them with me, if my cruel thoughts pursue me, I will come out—at least materially—of the scene in which I live. That is something."

My preparations for departure were not long. Whom had I to leave behind me? One person only, the one who bore my name, and it was from her I wished to fly. Perhaps I still cherished some vague hope. I said to myself that this journey would give her food for reflection; my presence near her had always placed me in the wrong; contrary to the proverb, my absence might right me.

My valet had just retired after packing my trunks, and I was putting my papers in order when my wife joined me.

"It is true then," she said, "I was not deceived, you are going on a journey?"

"As you see," I replied simply.

"Without telling me?"

"I would have said good-bye. I thought it unnecessary to agitate you beforehand."

She passed this irony unnoticed. Standing near the fire-place, her elbow leaning on the marble she watched me making my last preparations in silence. All at once, I heard her murmur these words:

"Yes, it is perhaps for the best."

I laid down the papers I held in my hand and advanced toward her.

"You think I am right in going away," I said. "My presence inconveniences you, does it not?"

"You mistake my meaning," she said gently; "my words contained nothing disparaging to you."

"Do you then hope that my absence will change your disposition toward me?"

She made no reply to this direct question; but after a few moments silence, she said:

"It is now winter; do you not fear the cold?"

"No, I am going South."

"When do you intend to return?" she asked.

"When you are to me what you should be." I replied.

I expected her to say: "I am a devoted companion, a faithful friend; I try to make your life agreeable; my disposition is charming, my temper always unruffled. What have you to find fault with in me?" and then, before my departure I would have given myself the sweet sweet satisfaction of retorting: "I did not marry you to make you a *dame de compagnie* and to admire your character. I render due homage to your intellectual qualities, but I should also like to know that you possess other qualities." In fact I would have said so much and more; I would have given vent to my indignation; that would have been some relief. But she did not furnish me the pretext; she may have dreaded my retorts and feared a scene, or she may have been really conscious of her wrongs toward me.

"It is time to go," I said at last.

I rang, ordered my trunks to be brought, and sent for a carriage.

While my orders were being executed I remained alone with her. We were looking at each other without exchanging a word; I leaning on the bookcase, she still standing near the chimney, her elbow on the marble, her head supported by her hand. The carriage stopped before the door, I made a step toward Paule.

"Good-bye," I said.

She advanced toward me and placed her brow within the reach of my lips, as a sister might have done in separating from her brother. But I was not her brother. I adored her, I adored her still in spite of all! During the hour she stood there in my chamber, so near me, I did not cease to admire her, notwithstanding my apparent coldness; a hundred times I repeated to myself; "How charming, how beautiful, how accomplished, how desirable she is!" And now my trembling lips pressed her burning brow. I felt the contact of her bosom against my breast; I felt her warm breath against my face. I could control myself no longer. With one arm I clasped her waist, trying to make her form yield, while I placed one hand on her head and my lips descended from her brow to her lips. Ah! if she had responded to this last embrace, to this last prayer; if a sigh had escaped from her lips, a breath; if she had but made an effort to evade my kisses, to defend herself, to struggle! No; faithful to her principles, she showed herself as she had always been; her form yielded in obedience to my touch, her head inclined under the pressure of my hand, her lips did not avoid mine; her whole person became insensible, inanimated, inert; she became galvanized, as it were. Instead of a woman, I held a corpse in my arms. Then all my ardors died away, and suddenly frozen by contact with this icy form, I fled.

XV

The day following my sad adieux, I was in Marseilles. Do not fear, my friend; I will not have the cruelty to make you travel with me, at any rate, you will probably refuse to follow me. Lovers are sad traveling companions; they sigh oftener than they admire, and I have known some who, in front of some wonderful sites or in a Musee resplendent with masterpieces, have sometimes closed their eyes, to better think and dream of their love.

At Marseilles I embarked for Italy. I visited or rather wandered through Rome, Naples, Florence, Venice, Milan, Turin, and taking the route of Corniche at Genes, I returned to France three months after my departure from it.

At Nice I stopped; before returning to Paris I desired to analyze the state of my heart and consult that of Paule. Alas! I was soon posted in regard to my own: this absence of three months, that wild run from city to city, had only accelerated its beatings. My imagination which, as you know, was already quite vagabond in Paris now abandoned itself to real disorderly sports. I had committed a great folly; when we wish to pacify, calm, and again become masters of ourselves, we should not take refuge in Italy, that classic land of volcanoes and secret Musees.

But what mattered this revival of ardors, if owing to my absence and the isolation in which she had lived Paule's heart was now in unison with mine? What do you say, my dear friend? On our return from Italy we are always full of hope. Spring had succeeded winter; I counted on the April sun to dissipate the mist that had risen between my wife and myself and melt the snows in the midst of which she had been pleased to live until now. "Everything around her at this moment sings of love," I said to myself; "she must be touched by this sublime harmony and anxious to mingle her voice with this grand concert of nature." Excuse the poetic tone of the last phrase; it is still Italy that inspires me. I shall now return to prose and leave it no more; for what remains to be told or rather to be guessed, does not merit a choice of style. In the face of certain infamies it is not permitted to be silent; the voice should be elevated to condemn them. Indifference, disdain, and silence encourage them; the shadow, the darkness that surrounds them, gives them hope of impunity; they spread, grow, prosper, they carry shame and dishonor with them. They must be combated openly, without fear of wounding delicate ears, of awakening dangerous ideas. It is by sparing vice, neglecting to blast it, through ridiculous modesty, that it sometimes passes for virtue. If you dare not tell the hunchback; "You have a hump," the dwarf, "You are deformed," this dwarf and hunchback will believe themselves handsome men. How many have been lost because there was not found a man strong enough, or with enough authority to cry out: "Beware! a new vice has just been hatched, a new leprosy has come into your midst!" Not being warned, they could not defend themselves; the vice grew, the leprosy extended, and made such ravages that each became impregnated with vice and leprosy and no longer saw the vice and leprosy of his neighbor.

But it is the duty of the narrator or the writer to signalize and stigmatize certain corruptions; and he must do so in one word or in one stroke of the pen. He cannot make long descriptions or too vivid paintings. That is why I said a few moments ago, with so much presumption, that the choice of style did not matter. You probably understand nothing of this violent outburst; it is a little premature, I must admit.

I resume my narrative where I left it. I reached Nice full of hope and enthusiasm. I wrote a touching letter to Paule—one of those epistles, so passionate that they communicate fire to their surroundings, and which we are tempted to consider dangerous to public safety when sent through the post. Three days later I received an answer. She had written by return mail; it was a good sign. I locked myself in my room and read it attentively; she did not answer one word to what I had said. Her letter contained no relation to mine. She spoke of her health which, she assured me, gave her cause of anxiety. She spoke of all she had done in Paris during the winter, the plays in vogue, the concerts and balls in course of preparation. I believe she even touched on one of the political questions of the day. In conclusion, she sent the compliments of her family and kissed me affectionately. She had—I must do her justice— filled four pages. It was long enough; I should have been satisfied, and would have been if, instead of enjoying the sad privilege of being her husband, fate had been pleased to make me her uncle. It was such a letter as we write to our grand-parents from school under the dictation or superintendence of the teacher. For the moment it was certainly useless to return to Paris; I decided to remain at Nice.

The *Hotel des Princes*, where I installed myself, is quite a distance from the center of the city and the English Promenade. But it faces the sea and commands an admirable view. As I was somewhat fatigued after my rapid journey, it possessed a precious advantage for me; it enjoyed perfect tranquillity. A great Russian lady, too delicate to be noisy, occupied the first floor, a few Englishmen had possession of the second, and I shared the third—reserved no doubt for France—with one of my compatriots. He was a man of about forty years, tall, thin, of sympathetic mien and distinguished manners.

The day after my arrival, chance placed me next to him at the dinner table. We first exchanged a few words of politeness, then conversed about our travels; he had just come from Italy also, where he had remained two years after wandering through Germany and the greater part of Russia. His conversation was most interesting; he had seen and studied everything. He spoke of foreign potentates as if he had been received at all the courts, and an instant later, described the morals and customs of the Caucasian peasants like a man who had long lived in their midst and even in their intimacy. A propos of morals, I remember a discussion that came up between us in our second conversation, while smoking our cigars after dinner in front of the hotel.

"Of all the people whom I have had the pleasure of studying," observed my companion, "the Frenchman is certainly the most dissolute in morals."

I protested.

"I assure you," he continued, "that we alone abandon ourselves to certain errors of imagination and to certain aberrations. In Germany, for instance, our refinements of corruption are almost unknown."

"I admit," I replied, "that in France, among the people, the peasants, morals leave a great deal to be desired, but in society, in the middle classes—"

"You are mistaken," he said interrupting me. "The black coat and the silk dress have in some way with us the privilege of depravity, and that explains itself; it is not the senses that are in question here, it is the imagination only. Luxury, idleness and reverie excite and drive it toward all species of errors. The peasants and workingmen have no time to dream, and if they had the time their imagination would not lend itself to it; they are too material to be corrupted, too naively sensual to be dissolute. They are robust, thanks to the atmosphere they breathe, the manual labor they perform; and corruption is generally the consequence of some physical weakness. We become dissolute as we become gourmands, in consequence of a want of appetite. The latter have recourse to new spices to be able to eat, the former perfect love to be able to love."

My companion talked long on this subject and I listened attentively. I had much to learn from such a master and especially such an observer. As I have often told you in the course of this narrative, my dear friend, and as you must moreover have perceived for yourself, notwithstanding my thirty odd years I was still an ingenue, a chaste one I might say, if the word were not applied to politics in our days. My youth, watched over by a most rigorous mother, the arduous labors to which I later abandoned myself, and certain natural dispositions that made me avoid dangerous companionships and pleasures, sufficiently explain the relative purity of my mind. My imagination had never gone beyond a certain limit, and it scarcely crossed its boundaries even now, notwithstanding the experience which my companion placed in my service. This may have been, because, as a man of good society he spoke in guarded terms, and his conversation was always marked by delicate reticence.

For several days we conversed in the same manner on subjects of which I had more knowledge and of which I could speak in an interesting way to my neighbor. We became almost inseparable. At ten o'clock breakfast united us; then we went for a walk on the road to Villefranche; at three we went to hear the music in the square where all Nicene society meets; dinner again brought us side by side, and in the evening we usually met at the *Cercle des Etrangers*, either in the reading or the card room.

Notwithstanding this intimacy, I was still in ignorance of my companion's name. I had heard him called Monsieur le Comte, several times by the proprietor or the waiters, but with that indifference which characterizes the traveler who knows that these relations, however charming they may be, cannot last, I had neglected to ask what name followed this title. One morning, I was suddenly enlightened on this subject and you will easily understand my surprise. I awakened with the presumptuous idea that the post would bring me a letter from Paule on that day. The hour of the distribution passed, and as no one seemed to think of bringing me my letter, I thought it might have been thrown into the glass box that contained the correspondence of strangers and I went down to the office. Naturally, I found no missive from my wife, and I was on the point of reproaching myself for my ingenuity, when my glance fell on a large envelope on which I read the following inscription:

Monsieur le Comte de Blangy,

Hotel des Princes, Nice.
(Alpes Maritimes)

This name of Blangy, which belonged to my wife's most intimate friend, could not fail to attract my attention; then the title of Monsieur le Comte by which the people of the hotel addressed my neighbor, suddenly recurred to me.

"Could his name be Blangy?" I asked myself. I was soon enlightened on this point, for a few minutes later the proprietor took the letter from under my eyes and handed it to a waiter with the order to carry it to No. 27. This was the room occupied by my neighbor. Then, as you may suppose, I asked myself if this de Blangy could be any relation to the countess. The orthography of the names and their titles were similar, besides divers particulars and remarks made on the character of my companion came to my mind. In all probability I had linked myself since my arrival at Nice, with the husband of Paule's friend.

Was it not said in society that he had been traveling for three years in foreign countries, and had not my companion declared on the previous day, that he experienced a great pleasure in seeing France again after three years' absence? Although he rarely spoke of himself he had once alluded to the time when he was in the diplomatic corps, and had I not heard that soon after his marriage the comte had placed his resignation in the hands of the Minister of Foreign Affairs? Moreover, his way of speaking of women, and the little respect they seemed to inspire in him, established his identity. It was indeed the language of the man who through lightness or a change of love, had acted so badly toward that poor Madame de Blangy and made a widow of her before she was scarcely married. For my first friendship contracted in traveling, I was certainly not very fortunate. But I soon admitted that M. de Blangy's conduct toward his wife was no concern of mine. Chance had given me an agreeable companion; I should rejoice and take advantage of my discovery to make our relations more intimate. "In an hour," I thought, "breakfast will bring us together and I will say graciously, 'If my good star had not brought us together at Nice, I should certainly have had the pleasure of meeting you this winter in Paris; for your wife and mine are intimate friends.'"

I had already repeated this phrase twice, endeavoring to round it off and polish it, when a thought suddenly struck me. "Why the idea is absurd!" I cried. "It is not to be supposed that M. de Blangy would care to speak of his wife. He has abandoned her and I have no reason to recall his troubles. He is trying to forget that he is married, and I certainly have no right to remind him of the fact."

Yes, decidedly, good taste commanded me to be silent. But for three months I had not spoken of Paule with a living soul, I had not once pronounced her name; a unique occasion now presented itself, and I was too much in love not to yield to the temptation in defiance of all propriety. I resisted for two days, however; I even believe that I could have resisted longer if Paule had had the good thought to write to me. I would have answered, unburdened my thoughts to her, and would then have found the strength to refrain from speaking. But nothing came; no letter, no word; absolute silence. Then, my dear friend, I became indiscreet and ridiculous, as you shall see. M. de Blangy and myself had just come out of the club-room and were entering the hotel for dinner, when after long puzzling my brain to find a way of broaching the subject, I said abruptly:

"While you were reading the papers, I amused myself by running over the register in which the members of the club are inscribed, and a familiar name struck me."

"Which?" he asked.

"M. de Blangy, the comte is then at Nice."

"Did you not know it?" he said, looking at me in astonishment.

"No, I did not. I know M. de Blangy by reputation, but have never met him."

"Are you sure?" he said smiling without a suspicion of what awaited him.

"I am quite certain."

"Permit me to say that you are mistaken. You have been with him continually for a week, and he congratulates himself sincerely on the fact."

As I still continued to appear astonished, that I might be faithful to my role, he added:

"I am the Comte de Blangy. I thought you knew it."

"No, I did not. I only knew that my good star had given me a polished and intelligent man for a companion. That sufficed me and I did not try to learn his name."

"We were wrong not to introduce ourselves," said the comte, "but we can make amends." And stepping on the walk he said laughingly; "I have the honor to present you M. de Blangy."

I introduced myself in my turn, but my name recalled nothing to him. This was not surprising since at the time of my marriage he had already left his wife and ceased all relations with her.

"You said you knew me by name," said the comte as we resumed our walk, "how do you explain that?"

This question was only natural and I expected it since I had provoked it. Nevertheless it troubled me. I felt that I was about to commit a blunder, but I had gone too far to recede.

"I have often heard my wife speak of you," I said, thinking it more delicate to speak of my wife than of his own.

"Ah! your wife knows me!"

"She met you in society before her marriage."

"Indeed? What was her maiden name?"

"Paule Giraud."

I had scarcely pronounced this name when I saw the comte turn pale and stagger. But before I could make a movement, he recovered himself and said coldly:

"Ah! you have married Mademoiselle Paule Giraud. It is true, I often met her in society; she is very pretty."

This was my opinion also, but I did not reply. We walked on some time in silence; then M. de Blangy seemed to recover his composure by a violent effort, stopped suddenly and said: "Does your wife still visit my wife?"

"They are inseparable," I replied.

He gave me a look that I shall remember all my life; he seemed to be trying to read my thoughts, to penetrate my soul. Then he turned his head away abruptly, and as we had reached the hotel, he left me, without a word, took the key of his room and disappeared. An hour later I went down to dinner but the comte aid not appear.

XVI

The next day I did not see him at all. On the second day we met on the English Promenade; but instead of hurrying toward me as he would have done two days previous, he merely raised his hat. This bow did not suffice me. I had a right to be astonished and offended by the abrupt change in his manners. Between well-bred people the past engages the future, and the bow of to-day does not replace the clasp of hands of yesterday. If I had fallen in his estimation, I had a right to expect and demand an explanation.

It was evident that I had displeased him in speaking of his wife; but his reserve toward me, in view of our old relations, bordered on impertinence, for my indiscretion did not justify it. The tone in which he had pronounced the words; "Ah! you have married Mlle. Giraud," had struck me. It was not merely an exclamation of surprise; I had discerned an accent of irony and stupefaction. Did a secret exist between my wife and the comte? Had he penetrated the mystery that I could not discover? Paule had conducted herself in such a strange manner toward me, she had placed me in such a false position, that I had a right to suspect and fear everything. I was not long in taking a decision: I resolved to see the comte as soon as possible, and to have a frank explanation with him.

As I have already said, we had met without exchanging a word. As soon as I had taken this resolution, I turned back. M. de Blangy was walking toward the hotel by the road along the sea. I followed at a distance. I saw him enter the hotel, and when I had waited long enough to give him time to go to his room, I ascended in my turn and knocked at his door.

"Come in!" said a voice.

I turned the knob and entered.

"Ah! it is you, monsieur!" exclaimed the comte unable to conceal his vexation.

"Yes, monsieur, it is I," I replied. "I am sorry to disturb you but it is necessary that we should have a moment's conversation. You no longer come to the table d'hote, and you seem disposed to walk by yourself, therefore, I am obliged to commit the indiscretion of coming to your door."

"I am at your service, monsieur," said the comte. "Pray be seated."

He pointed to a chair, seated himself opposite me and awaited the explanation of my visit.

"Monsieur," I resumed in a voice that I tried to render calm, but which was much agitated, "I was congratulating myself on my good relations with you since the day we met in the hotel, when those good relations suddenly ceased. I am in ignorance of the reasons which can have made you pass abruptly from great amiability to entire reserve. And I come to ask you frankly for those reasons."

"The reserve to which you make allusion, monsieur," replied the comte, "has nothing personal to you. I beg you to attribute it to grave preoccupations that have suddenly assailed me."

"If it were merely a question of cicatrizing a wound to my self-love," I said, "this answer would satisfy me. But my self-love is not engaged here. Permit me to appeal to your indulgence. We had passed the greater part of the day together, we were conversing cheerfully together, we had even just presented ourselves to each other and cemented our friendship, when I accidentally pronounced my wife's maiden name; immediately, your voice, your looks, your manners became metamorphosed; in front of the hotel you took leave of me with an abruptness which is not habitual to you, and since then you have not spoken to me. Pray put yourself an instant in my place. Would you not say, there is evidently some mystery, some secret which I should know?"

"There is neither mystery nor secret, monsieur," said the comte.

"Do you give me your word for it?" I asked.

"But—"

"You hesitate? That suffices. I was not mistaken."

M. de Blangy tried to protest against this quick manner of interpreting his hesitation, but I gave him no time.

"Will you satisfy a very legitimate curiosity," I rejoined, "and aid me in penetrating the mystery in question?"

"Ah! monsieur," cried the comte rising, "I repeat it, there is no mystery."

"You will remark," I insisted, "that I came to have a peaceful and courteous explanation. Now it is a prayer I address you, and that you may accede to it I appeal to our former relations, our pleasant conversations, and the sympathy we felt toward each other."

He seemed moved, and for an instant I thought he would yield to my prayers.

"No, no, I have nothing to say!" he cried suddenly.

"This is your last word?"

"Yes, it is my last word."

"You are wrong, monsieur," I said firmly.

"Why?" he asked raising his head haughtily.

"Oh," I cried, "because I am in one of those positions in which we have nothing to spare, in which we spare nothing, in which we are ready for everything, decided to everything."

He looked at me with more astonishment than irritation, and advancing toward me, he said:

"Take care; you assured me you had entered my room with pacific intentions; your words are now almost a menace."

"I am not menacing. I am praying with animation, with urgency, praying an honest man to explain himself frankly. It is your own fault, Monsieur le Comte; for this scene would not have taken place if you had been more master of yourself the other day and concealed your impressions. Through your fault I repeat, I am perhaps on the track of a secret I have long searched in vain. Well, I want to know this secret. I must know it."

M. de Blangy did not seem wounded by my words but merely said:

"Ah! you have long searched for a secret?"

"Yes," I cried losing my head entirely, "a secret on which depends my happiness. My life is wearing itself out in searching it; I am the most unhappy of men—and you, monsieur, you who by one word might put an end to my sufferings, yes, you who could have told me all since I entered, and restored to me my tranquillity, you refuse to explain. Ah, it is wrong I repeat it, to treat as an enemy a man reduced to despair. A man whose life is a burden to him, and—"

"And you would willingly expose that life in a duel."

"Oh! yes!" I cried.

He took a step toward me and said:

"Then we would be both fighting because of your wife, would we not?"

"My wife!"

"No doubt," he replied, becoming excited in his turn. "If you are unhappy, if life is a burden to you, is it not because of her? Do you think that I have not guessed it? Ah, monsieur, if you have married Mademoiselle Giraud, I have married her friend. If you travel for three months far from your wife, I travel for many years far from mine!" He paused, seemed to reflect, and resumed in a calmer tone. "The step you have undertaken, the sincerity that I read in your eyes, the half confidences that have escaped you, and the avowal of your grief, are for me so many proofs that I am in the presence of a noble man. For an instant, I doubted you; you will learn the reason later, and I beg you sincerely to pardon me."

I bowed in silence, and he continued:

"You pretend that I am in possession of a secret which must interest you. I admit it. But my conscience forbids me to unveil it unless compelled to it. A few moments ago you alluded to the grief you felt. I must know its exact nature. It may have no relation to the secret in question, and then neither your prayers nor threats can tear it from me. If, on the contrary, in unveiling it I can bring consolation to your sorrows, give you warning and advice, I give you my word that I will explain myself in the most precise manner. You must therefore decide if you think me worthy of your confidence. Exchange your secret for mine; if, I repeat it, it is necessary that you should know it. This is my last word."

Could I hesitate? The man who proposed to unfold the secret of my life, was, after all, the husband of my wife's best friend, the woman who for so many years had been the confidante of her most intimate thoughts. Mme. de Blangy was not perhaps the only one who knew the motive of Paule's conduct toward me; the comte had no doubt also guessed it. Had he not received Mlle. Giraud in his own house before separating from his wife? It was not astonishing that he should know certain particulars which I did not. Chance now placed me in the presence of the only person who could unveil the secret, and, through a false shame, an exaggerated delicacy, was I to refuse these necessary confidences which I had myself solicited?

No; I spoke in all sincerity, as I speak to you, my dear friend. I related all the sad incidents of my campaign of love, sparing none of the details.

He listened in silence, grave and thoughtful. One could almost have believed that my story was his own, that my adventures had happened to him, so much did he seem interested. "Yes, that is it; I recognize her; always the same!" were the exclamations with which he interrupted my confidences now and then.

I had just told him how curiosity and jealousy had led me to follow my wife to Rue Laffitte, and had reached the moment when seeing her come out of the apartments, I rushed toward the door, pushed her aside, and found myself face to face with—

"Madame de Blangy!" cried the comte.

"What! you have guessed it!" I cried in astonishment.

"Have I guessed it? What surprises me is that you were astonished. What! you had visited these apartments the day before and did not suspect it?"

"But," I replied innocently, "how could I suspect that these ladies would rent apartments to meet and visit each other?"

The comte knitted his brow and looked at me. He has since told me that at the time, he really suspected me of making sport of him. My innocent air, however, and the frankness of my physiognomy reassurred him.

"Pray continue," he said.

"I have nothing of interest to add," I replied. "Madame de Blangy invited me to enter her bachelor apartments, as she called them, Paule followed me, and they explained that in consequence of my orders not to see each other again, they had been compelled to make a rendezvous in Rue Laffitte."

"And then!" cried the comte, "you did not protest, you did not show your indignation?"

"Mon Dieu!" I said, "in seeing her friend, my wife was indeed guilty of rebellion against my authority; but for three days I had suspected her of such a grave crime that I never dreamed of complaining of a simple disobedience. Remember, monsieur, that I expected to find a rival, a lover, and I found myself face to face with a charming and well-bred woman."

"Are you speaking seriously?" asked the comte taking another step toward me.

"Certainly."

"You congratulated yourself in finding your wife with mine in those apartments in the Rue Laffitte?"

"I did not congratulate myself, but I preferred this discovery to the other one I had expected to make."

"Ah! monsieur, I am not of your opinion," exclaimed the comte, "I would have preferred to avenge myself?"

"Vengeance," I replied, "certainly has something in its favor, and I swear I had thought of it more than once. But you must admit that it was more agreeable to say: 'I believed I was deceived and I am not; my wife is not guilty.'"

These last words, pronounced in the most innocent way in the world, were a revelation to M. de Blangy. He could no longer doubt my perfect candor.

His surprise was so complete that the comte found it difficult to open my eyes. My conscience for a time revolted and refused to believe what I heard. There exist minds so constructed that certain thoughts cannot enter, much less engrave themselves there. Notwithstanding my natural honesty which had caused me to evade unhealthful confidences, notwithstanding the exceptional existence which had sheltered me from all dangerous spectacles, I was not without some vague intuition of all our miseries; but I believed, in good faith, that birth and education had elevated a barrier between certain classes of society and such wretchedness.

M. de Blangy insisted that such a state existed among the people and the middle classes only as exceptions, but I refused to believe in these exceptions. I was however, forced to be convinced by the evidence. Seduced by the dazzling beauty of Paule's friend, by her wit and originality, the comte had, like myself, made a marriage of inclination. But he was less guilty than I had been, for far from imitating Mlle. Giraud's frankness, M. de Blangy's fiancee had, on the contrary, brought into action all the seductions with which nature had endowed her to induce the comte to give her his name and fortune. I must do her the justice to say, however, that she did not conduct herself toward M. de Blangy exactly as Paule conducted herself toward me. The comte had certainly an incontestable advantage over me; she placed no bolt on her door and did not seem to have pronounced any vows. But he was not slow in perceiving her coldness. Her reserve and indifference were so complete that M. de Blangy became seriously alarmed. Like me, he one day asked himself if Mme. de Blangy were not perhaps economical in her conjugal affections, that she might commit culpable prodigalities. He followed her, saw her enter a house in the Rue Louis-le-Grand, bribed the concierge, concealed himself in the apartments and succeeded in hearing the conversation between his wife and the woman who, alas! was destined to be mine later. What he heard in this conversation, in which marriage was boldly assailed, tickled his ears so disagreeably that he could not restrain his indignation. He appeared at the moment when they were speaking the most ill of him. Paule, in her quality of young girl, blushed, turned pale and ended by having a nervous attack. As to the countess, she paid him back in audacity; she retracted nothing he had heard, and even had the effrontery to glorify herself in her subversive ideas.

During the dissipated life he had led before marriage, the comte had often heard strange theories upheld, but he now stood confounded, overwhelmed. Indignation gave place to stupefaction, anger to scorn; he knew not what to answer. He had not the strength to punish. Punish! How could he?

"Justice," continued the comte, "would certainly have refused its assistance. The legislator has not provided for certain faults, and impunity is assured them. It would even have been difficult to obtain a separation; Madame de Blangy's wrongs toward me were of such nature that judges often refuse to admit them, that they may not be forced to brand them. Moreoever, what proof had I to offer? What testimony could I invoke? That of Mademoiselle Paule Giraud? She was too much interested in the debate for her word to be taken in consideration; and beside she would have died rather than compromise her friend. She is an unconquerable creature whom my wife alone has had the power to dominate. Must I then act for myself? Ah! monsieur, in such cases men of our sphere have no resource. Brutality, violence, is repugnant to them. They shrink before the scandal that would surround their name; they fear the ridicule they cannot escape. I have seen my club companions pursue with their railleries poor husbands deceived in the ordinary way; would I have found mercy in their eyes because of the singular and exceptional position in which I was placed? No, they would have laughed at me without even dreaming of blaming Mme. de Blangy. In Parisian society of the nineteenth century, we are pleased, through lightness of character and love of paradox, to scoff at the victim and exonerate the guilty one. It is thus that vice of all kinds, sure of impunity, often of protection even, filters little by little into our morals."

I admit, my dear friend, that I was not listening to M. de Blangy's recriminations against modern society; the confidence he had just made alone occupied me.

"But!" I cried in a moment of lucidity, "you at least forbade them to meet again; you tried to separate them?"

"Certainly I tried," replied M. de Blangy, "but do you think that a man who respects himself can long be the spy and jailer of his wife? This surveillance of every instant in time fatigues, disgusts and wears out the firmest will, the most deeply rooted energy."

"Why did you not oblige your wife to travel with you? This watchfulness would have been unnecessary in foreign parts"

"You are in error; the first time I should have left her alone at the hotel, she would have darted away like an arrow, taken the first train for Paris and rejoined her inseparable friend."

"But," I cried energetically, "if Madame de Blangy had known that she would not find her friend in Paris, if while you dragged your wife away on a voyage, Mlle. Giraud had been suddenly torn away from the Rue Caumartin, if while you directed yourself toward America with one, the other had been taken toward Russia, without telling them of the direction you intended to follow, where and at what time would they have met again?"

I paused to see the effect my idea produced on the comte.

"Who would have had the will and power to tear Mlle. Giraud from Paris? and keep her wandering over the world against her will for an unlimited period?" he asked. "Neither her father nor mother assuredly."

Deeply impressed with my subject, I interrupted him.

"Ah, monsieur le comte, I am not speaking of what you should have done in other days, but of what you could do to-day. If the law commands Madame de Blangy to follow you wherever you will, if it gives you the means to compel her, does it not also give me the same rights over Mlle. Giraud, since I am her husband? She is no longer a young girl, dependent on her family, but a married woman, dependent on me. Nothing prevents us from leaving this evening or to-morrow for Paris, stop at a hotel to conceal our arrival, make the preparation for a long journey, secretly and speedily; if necessary dispose of securities that we may not be stopped on the way by the miserable question of money; if need be evoke the law and obtain the legal means of being obeyed by our wives. Ah, monsieur! the time for delicacy and sentiment is past. The law protects us; let us take advantage of it? Once the preparations are terminated, all formalities gone through, then we will clasp each other's hand and say adieu. Two carriages will convey us to the Rue Caumartin, one will stop at your door, the other at mine. We will enter, and giving our wives no time to see each other, to write or exchange a sign, we shall drag them away. They may perhaps resist. Well, then, monsieur, are we not determined, and shall we not have foreseen everything? If need be we shall use force and compel them to follow us. The day following our irruption into our respective domiciles, carried away by two express trains going in contrary directions, we shall find ourselves two hundred leagues apart—what do you think of my project?"

"It might succeed."

"Certainly, it would."

"But," resumed the comte after a moment's reflection, "you have been separated from your wife scarcely four months, I have been separated from mine more than three years. Your misfortune is recent, your wounds are still open, mine have closed long ago. In other days, I would perhaps have accepted your proposition with enthusiasm; to-day I refuse it because I no longer love."

"You no longer love!" I exclaimed. "Then why do you persist in this voluntary exile? why do you not return to Paris where your tastes, habits, career, relations recall you? Why vegetate here when you can live over there?"

He bowed his head and did not reply. Emboldened by this first success, I continued in these terms:

"Admit that you do not love. Scorn has killed love in us both. Our wives have become entirely indifferent to us. They do not deserve the trouble we shall take to reconquer them. But in the name of morality, which you invoked a little while ago; when you branded with indignation the people who do not condemn and punish certain errors. And yet, they of whom you speak were not interested as we are in the suppression. Will you reserve all your anger for others, and accord yourself a plenary indulgence? No, monsieur, no, we owe it to society, we owe it to ourselves, to do justice to this guilty misconduct."

I went on for a long time in this strain. Ah, my dear friend, I was no longer the young married man whom you have known full of delicacy, reserve, innocence and modesty, passing his life in solving an unsolvable enigma. Light had dawned upon me. I knew, I saw.

XVII

Three days after the conversation, I reached Paris accompaned by the count, and took refuge in a hotel of the Rue du Bac. We thought it prudent to place the Seine between ourselves and our wives that we might not be exposed to the chance of a meeting. We went by carriage everywhere and implored the discretion of the persons we were obliged to see.

We displayed so much activity in our purchases, our realization of funds, and our different undertakings that forty-eight hours after our arrival in Paris we were ready to leave it and prepared to compel our wives to follow us.

"Shall it be this evening?" I asked the count, as I rejoined him at about four o'clock in the afternoon at the hotel.

"Very well let it be this evening. Nothing hinders us and I am in a hurry to have it over. What route do you take that I may choose mine? It is an important point to settle."

"Pray fix your itinerary, I shall settle mine afterward."

"If you see no obstacles," replied M. de Blangy, "I shall direct myself toward the north; I shall go straight before me, but cannot say at what points I shall stop."

"It is not necessary that I should know. You have chosen the north, I choose the south; I will take the express for Marseilles or Bordeaux, it matters not which, this very night."

"You must then reach either of the two stations at eight o'clock."

"I shall reach it."

"In that case there remains but to say adieu, wish each other good luck and start for the Rue Caumartin."

"I agree with you."

We then ordered two carriages, had our luggage brought down and took leave of each other. We clasped hands warmly; we had learned to love and esteem each other many days ago.

At six o'clock my carriage stopped in front of my door. I alighted quickly, and without asking any information of the concierge, ascended the stairs, opened the door of my apartments and entered the drawing-room. My heart was beating violently; but I was calm in appearance, and determined.

Paule was seated near the chimney with a book on her lap. As she saw me she uttered a cry of surprise, arose and came to meet me with outstretched hands. I did not advance mine.

"Why," she said in astonishment, "are you not going to say good day to me after four months of separation?"

I did not answer, but continued to look at her. She had not changed much since I had left her; her fresh color had disappeared, the blood seemed to have withdrawn from the lips formerly so red, her cheeks were hollow, and a bluish ring encircled her eyes. Her form was more slender, and in spite of the ample garment she wore, one could not help seeing the emaciation of her whole person.

"Why do you look at me like that?" she asked.

"I find you very much changed," I replied.

"That is possible. I have been suffering lately with neuralgia and palpitation of the heart. Nervousness, no doubt. But what an odd way you have of greeting me."

"I begin by noticing the state of your health. Is not that natural? You must be treated."

"Dictate your orders," she said smiling, "since you have returned as a doctor."

"You must have a change of air," I rejoined, "travel and take exercise."

"Really? I will reflect on your prescription, doctor, and perhaps follow your advice in a few days."

"You must follow it this very day."

"What! to-day?"

"Yes, I give you one hour to prepare yourself for departure."

And without looking at her, without seeming to notice her astonishment, I walked to the chimney and pulled the bell. A maid appeared.

"Madame leaves this evening for a journey," I said to the girl. "Place in her trunk her most indispensable articles of toilet. She will join you in an instant and help you. Go and be quick."

"But you are mad, monsieur," cried Paule when the maid had gone.

"I have never been more sane," I replied.

"And you believe that I will go like this, suddenly, in obedience to your caprice?"

"Oh, it is not a caprice, it is a firm and immovable will."

"It is not a question of my health then; admitting that I am ill, you could not have known it beforehand."

"I knew you to be seriously attacked morally; that was sufficient. I have just learned that you also suffer physically, and I am the more determined to execute my projects."

"What are your projects. I know them only in part."

"You know them entirely. You leave Paris this evening at eight o'clock."

"Really? and I go alone?"

"No. I accompany you."

"Oh, it does not suffice you to travel; you must make others travel also."

"You are right."

"And where will you take me?"

"I do not know."

"How delightful!" she cried, bursting into a laugh.

I waited until this access of nervous gayety was passed, and resumed with the greatest calm. "Permit me to observe that the time is going fast. If you give no instructions to your maid, you will probably miss many things that you may need when we reach the hotel to-morrow, after a night's travel."

"I have no instructions to give," she said sitting down. "I am not going."

"I beg your pardon," I replied. "You are going, willingly or by force."

"By force!" she exclaimed.

"Yes, by force. All my arrangements are complete. Here," I continued drawing a paper from my pocket, "I have but to send this letter two steps from here to M. Bellanger who is officially ordered to place himself at my disposal. You may not know M. Bellanger; he is nevertheless well known in this quarter. Believe me, do not oblige me to disturb him; and make your preparations gracefully."

She looked at me, reflected a moment, then suddenly understanding the gravity of the situation she came to a decision.

"Very well, then we shall travel," she said slowly. "You command it and the law gives you the right; but I cannot go this evening. I have adieux to make."

"To whom?" I asked.

"To my father and mother."

"They will be here in a few minutes as I have notified them of your departure. Whom else do you want to see?"

"Madame de Blangy."

"I expected this," I said, losing a little of my calmness. "Well, Madame de Blangy has not time to receive your adieux. She also starts off on a long journey this evening."

"Berthe? Impossible!" she cried. "You are deceiving me."

"Why should she not go? Are you not going?"

"To begin with, I am not going; and beside she has not the misfortune to be in her husband's power as I am."

"Really? Is the comte then dead?"

"He might as well be since she does not know what has become of him."

"I can enlighten you on that point. At this moment he is a few steps from here, in the Rue Caumartin, on the second floor in his own apartments. He is informing his wife of his projects which are entirely similar to mine. He is expressing his wishes, she refuses to submit, then he tells her: 'I will shrink before nothing—nothing—do you hear? neither before scandal nor violence. You will follow me since I wish you to do so.' And she will follow him because one does not resist a man as determined as M. de Blangy, a man who has terrible weapons against his wife and against you?"

At these words she turned pale and bowed her head.

"You understand me, do you not?" I continued, becoming more and more excited as I went on. "I met M. de Blangy at Nice; we became friends and exchanged confidences. I know what influence the countess exercises over your mind. I have sworn to tear you from it. M. de Blangy has promised to second my efforts, and we are men of our word. Now believe me, arise and prepare yourself to follow me."

Confused, crushed, uncertain as to what she should do, she still remained seated. At this moment I heard the door-bell and I came nearer.

"It is your mother," I said, "who comes to bid you farewell. No recriminations, no complaints, or I warn you I will complain in my turn and explain the reasons that force me to drag you away from Paris."

"Oh! you would not do that?" she cried, rising.

"I have told you that I would recoil before nothing—nothing—do you hear? You must follow me immediately. If you hesitate another instant I shall speak and afterward act."

"Very well, I will follow you," she said in a low voice.

M. and Mme. Giraud entered. I explained their daughter's sudden departure; a provincial relative was very ill, I had just spent a few days at his bed-side and he begged me to bring my wife as soon as possible that he might see her before he died.

Paule confirmed this fable, kissed her father and mother, promised to return soon and went into her dressing-room. I followed her. The comte and I had agreed to watch our wives constantly until the hour of departure, that they might have no chance to write to each other.

Paule, who now seemed resigned, gave some orders to her maid, took different objects from a cupboard, placed them hastily in a satchel, threw a shawl over her shoulders and covering her head with a small traveling toque turned to me and said:

"I am at your service."

She went down and I followed closely, watching all her movements. My carriage was awaiting us at the door. I opened it and assisted Paule to enter. Then assuring myself that there was no one near, I went to give some orders to the servant who was assisting the coachman in placing our luggage. As I turned back a minute later, I saw a woman in a cap rapidly crossing the street. I recongized her; she was Mme. de Blangy's maid. While I was watching the sidewalk she had come to the middle of the street and exchanged a few words with Paule at the door of the carriage.

What could they have said? It was useless to question my wife on the subject. I took my place at her side, and cried to the coachman loud enough to be heard by everybody; "Gare Montparnasse!" The carriage rolled off in the direction of the boulevard, and as we came out of the Rue Caumartin we met a carriage which I thought I recognized as the one in which the comte had come to his wife's house two hours previous. Our double expedition had succeeded. In the Rue Rivoli I leaned out of the window and changed my first orders to the coachman. A few minutes before eight we reached the Gare de Lyon. I bought two tickets for Marseilles and we took our places in the express.

XVIII

My conversation with Paule from Paris to Marseilles was, as you may easily understand, not of the most animated. The situation between us was too strained to allow us to converse on commonplace subjects, and I had no inclination to resume the conversation interrupted by the arrival of M. and Mme. Giraud. I had told Paule all I had to say; she knew I was incensed by her conduct, and I had concealed the indignation she inspired in me. Besides I was not a man to wage incessant and continual war, to unceasingly direct against her the arms that M. de Blangy's revelations had placed in my hands, to overwhelm her with eternal wrath. My love had resisted the blow it had received and I became in a measure the accomplice of my wife's fault. I was, therefore, not in a state to reproach her; and the scorn which I might have displayed toward her would have recoiled on me in part. I decided, through respect for myself, never to allude to the facts, to forget as far as it was possible and to create a new life for Paule as well as for myself. Should you accuse me of being too indulgent in pardoning the injuries I had received, I would answer that you cannot be a judge in my case. I was not indulgent; I loved, that was my excuse. What! did my love still survive? Ah! this is what may astonish you and with which you have a right to reproach me. But your astonishment will never equal mine; and as to reproaches I heaped them upon myself.

Do not believe, however, that I was preparing to give free scope to that love, to again pursue the one who inspired it and to profit by the advantages given me by the rigorous measures I had taken. No, I would control myself, I would wait; was I not used to it? Notwithstanding my culpable attachment, I still had a sentiment of dignity; it would not have been to my credit to display my weakness before Paule, and to change from one day to the other, without transition, in my manner toward her. I wanted to give her imagination time to calm itself, to realize and understand her errors and to blush for them.

A prey for many years to pernicious advice and calamitous examples, bent under a diabolical domination, unconscious of her wrongs, blinded, infatuated, she needed time to regain her liberty, to reconquer her independence, that light might dawn in her mind and in her heart. There was a soul to save, and I would save it. If you find me ridiculous, so much the worse for you.

Thanks to the fast express, there is scarcely any distance between Paris and Marseilles. My intention, therefore, was not to remain in that city, where I should have been forced to exercise an incessant watchfulness over Paule to prevent her from returning to Rue Caumartin. I was determined to continue my journey by embarking on the first vessel that left port.

If, according to his program, M. de Blangy had taken his wife toward the north, that is, in the direction of England, the Channel and Mediterranean would soon separate the two friends, and then I could without presumption allow my hopes to revive. When we reached Marseilles, I took a carriage and ordered the coachman to drive straight to the port.

A steamer was making preparations for departure. I went in search of information and learned that the ship's destination was Oran. It would sail at five o'clock, and being Wednesday, would reach port Friday night or Saturday morning. I then rejoined my wife.

"If you consent," I said, pointing to the ship, "we shall embark on that steamer."

"You do not need my consent," she replied. "Do with me as you will."

She alighted from the carriage, took my arm, and we were soon installed with our baggage. After a favorable voyage, we reached the port of Oran Saturday morning. We were conducted to the Hotel de la Paix, on the Place Kleber, where we secured very comfortable apartments consisting of two bedrooms separated by a large parlor. You see, my dear friend, that I did not abuse the situation; I was resigned to live a bachelor life on the coast of Africa as I had done in Paris. If I had placed two seas between Paule and Mme. de Blangy, I had—at least for a time—the discretion of placing two thick walls between my wife and myself.

I will give you the least possible details of my sojourn in Oran; in my disposition of mind, I cared little for the city in which chance had placed me, or its inhabitants. I had but one thought; to amuse my wife, change the course of her ideas, efface the past in her mind, give her a taste for a new life and strive to please her.

This was no easy matter, I assure you. Not, however, that Paule—as I had feared—was obstinate in refusing all distractions and pleasure, for she seemed indifferent on the subject. She did not ever appear angry with me for the violence I had shown toward her, and in many instances I had occasion to see that none of my delicacies passed unperceived and that she was grateful for my attentions. But she was usually plunged in a sort of prostration, very difficult to conquer in spite of her real, visible efforts. At first I believed she was ill morally only, and that she suffered from the abrupt change in her life. But I soon realized that she was also ill physically, and that a complete perturbation had taken place in her health. The emaciation I had noticed on my return to Paris continued to increase; her eyes became more brilliant, the pupils more dilated; she complained of palpitations, difficulty in breathing, violent neuralgic pains in the head and heart, and at night I often heard from my room a dry, hacking cough. Indeed she was unceasingly a prey to a multitude of phenomena and nervous spasms caused by a general weakening of the system.

She realized her state of health and seemed alarmed; and when I proposed to see a physician she immediately consented. Doctor X—, whom I consulted, had long been celebrated among his colleagues in Paris, but he had been forced to abandon his large practice and settle in Africa on account of his health. Although he has since recovered, he still remains in Oran, where he has married and practices his profession to the great joy of the French colony. I accompanied my wife to the doctor's home; he examined her carefully, seemed to study the case with extreme attention, and gave a prescription without explaining the nature of her illness. But as we took leave of him he intimated that he would like to see me again. An hour later I was tete-a-tete with him in his study.

"The state of your wife is quite serious," he said. "I believe it my duty to warn you."

"What is the name of her malady?" I asked with emotion.

"She has no very pronounced malady at present, but she is in a state of chloro-anæmia which demands to be energetically fought."

"Let us fight it, then, doctor; with your assistance I am sure of victory."

"You are mistaken," he replied. "I can do but little and you can do all."

"I!"

"Yes, you. Will you allow me to ask you a few questions, although you are not the patient?"

"Go on, doctor."

"What existence did you lead in your early manhood?"

"The most laborious and least dissipated of existences."

"I suspected as much. You did not live in *petit-creve*, if I may use an expression which has come in vogue in Paris since I left it. You have not wasted your health. You have preserved yourself fresh and sound; then in the strength of your manhood you married the woman of your choice, a very pretty woman indeed! How long have you been married?"

"Almost one year," I said sadly.

"I suspected it. You are young married people."

This conversation was beginning to annoy me.

"What conclusion do you draw from my answers doctor?" I asked.

"Oh! you understand me very well," he replied, "we are young, ardent, loving, we fear nothing, we do not reflect that certain feminine natures need much delicacy and care. You see, my dear monsieur, young girls brought up in large cities, as your wife has been, that is in a hot-house, deprived of sun and pure air, should never be loved too ardently. If passion charms, it also kills them, because they have not been prepared for it. A husband, in certain cases, must curb his passion and place a check on his affections."

"According to you," I said smiling bitterly, "I have not placed a check on mine?"

"The examination I have just made of your wife indicatas it sufficiently. I do not make it a crime in you; you sinned through ignorance; but in mercy, now that you are warned, be more considerate."

And it was to me that such language was addressed! To me! I was accused of wanting in delicacy to my wife! I promised the doctor not to be selfish. What could I say? I could not unveil all my misery to him.

"At least, do you promise to cure your patient?" I asked.

"I hope so if the cause of her illness is removed. But bear in mind that her state of health is serious and might be followed by cerebral disorders. If care is not exercised, she will slowly drift into what in my day was called, *peri-meningo encephalite diffuse* and which is now briefly designated under the name of *pachy-meningite*."

These technical terms were not calculated to reassure or cheer me. I took leave of the doctor, fearing that once started he would never stop. Was I not sufficiently enlightened on the state of Paule's health? Thanks to this voyage, I was to be her savior physically as well as morally.

XIX

Outside of the personal recommendations—so easily observed—made by Doctor X—the treatment prescribed to Paul was very simple. She must take a great deal of exercise, live in the open air, and amuse herself as much as possible. There was nothing therefore to detain us at Oran and prevent me from following to the letter the plans which M. de Blangy and myself had laid out and which consisted in never remaining more than one week in the same place. We made very interesting excursions along the coast and in the interior; and I took away all Paule's chances of communicating with France, and above all of receiving letters, by my constant vigilance. But on our second visit to the doctor, he advised my wife to try the efficacy of the hot-springs situated at three kilometers from Oran and known as the Queen's baths, in remembrance of the wonderful cure of Isabella's daughter, the princess Jeanne, in the days of Spanish dominion.

We therefore settled in Oran; I rented a caleche to convey us every morning to the bathing establishment, and took in my service an intelligent looking little Arab of twelve or thirteen years of age—a yaouley as they are called—answering to the name of Ben-Kader. Our time passed very agreeably; from the baths we went to breakfast at Saint André, a picturesque maritime village, and after an hour or two of rest we usually undertook the ascent of the little town of Mersel-Kebir, on the summit of which stands a celebrated fortress from which we enjoyed an admirable view. Sometimes after leaving the bath, we returned to Oran by the most direct route. The afternoon was then devoted to excursions in the city and principally to the Promenade de Letang, where we had for horizon the immensity of the Mediterranean.

Ben-Kader followed us constantly, always ready to assist us or give us information in the *patois* which the little Arabs use to make themselves understood by the French.

"You know, you, monsieur, the lady went over there, in the street," he would say when he saw me looking for Paule who had absented herself from the hotel for a few instants.

The fact is that Ben-Kader knew a great deal more of what passed in the street than in the hotel where he entered only at his peril. The yaouley has an instinctive horror of the ceilings and interior walls of a house. He must have open air, space, the blue sky above his head.

Scarcely covered by loose pantaloons and a calico vest confined to the waist by a red belt, bare-footed, the head adorned by a fez, his principal occupation consists in sitting down on the walks of the squares or frequented street and taking care of horses.

As soon as an officer sets foot on the ground at the door of a cafe, a crowd of yaouley surround him. He usually recognizes his favorite and confides the horse to his care. The little Arab instead of taking the bridle, sits down before the horse and talks to him. The animal, habituated to this fashion, awaits his master patiently, sometimes for several hours in company with his guardian. When the cavalier returns, the yaouley without rising cries: "You know, you monsieur, give me two *sous*."

The two *sous* are thrown and he is enraptured; his day's work is done. Whether Paule often gave Ben-Kader two *sous* or had the talent of making his conquest, I know not; but what is positive is that he obeyed her much better than he did me and he seemed entirely devoted to her.

After dinner, I usually spent half an hour at the Cafe Soubiran and afterward joined my wife in the parlor that separated our two rooms. While she occupied herself with embroidery, I read aloud from some good book which I had chosen for her edification. The evenings were spent in this manner and at ten o'clock we retired to our respective chambers. This life, active during the day, intellectual in the evening, free from all anxiety, had a happy influence on Paule's health; she recovered her strength, the color came back to her cheeks little by little, and she was regaining some of the embonpoint she had formerly possessed. From a moral point of view, she also seemed improved. As you are aware, I had promised, through delicacy, never to address her one reproach on the subject of her conduct toward me and never to refer to the past. But sometimes during our readings, a line, a word, recalled our respective situations and seemed an allusion to them. Then Paule, who in other days would not have been troubled, would blush and lower her eyes. One evening she had hazarded certain reflections which I cannot pass in silence. We were reading the first pages of a novel in which the author, having spoken of the heroine's childhood, was beginning to entertain us by her girlhood and the education that was prepared for her.

"Provided they don't send her to a boarding-school!" cried Paule suddenly.

This remark stopped me short in my reading.

"You believe boarding-schools dangerous for a young girl?" I said.

"They may be," she replied.

"What kind of education do you prefer?"

"That which is received under the eyes of her mother, in her own home."

"It is not always easy for a mother to bring up her daughter well."

"Then let her bring her up ill; but let her bring her up herself by all means; in default of instructions she will at least give her sentiments of honesty."

"Do you also exclude private schools?"

"I admit small schools with a limited number of scholars."

"Why?"

"Because the teachers can then exercise a more active, more motherly watchfulness over the pupils. I have nothing to reproach in large schools in the matter of education, but they are open to three or four hundred young girls of all ages and conditions. The little ones are separated from the older ones, they may say. To begin with, this is not entirely true; they are thrown together on many occasions; they are united and converse freely together. Besides, what are the older and little ones? Those ranging from ten to thirteen and those that hover between fifteen and seventeen. This is how they are usually classed, and it is absurd; at thirteen some girls are morally old, and many girls of seventeen deserve to be classed among the little ones. They make a material classification, classic so to say, when prudence demands a moral classification. What is the consequence? The innocent ones are brought in continual contact with those who are no longer so, and they soon lose their candor and purity of soul. In small private schools, the teachers are more intimate with their pupils, they converse with them, receive their confidences, know their faults, and can keep the black sheep from their flock; if they are honest women they exercise a good influence over those young hearts. In large schools the teachers are no doubt equally excellent women and animated by good intentions, but their influence is too much disseminated to be exercised usefully."

She paused.

"Then you believe that a young girl brought up away from home can not make a true wife?" I said.

"Great Heavens!" she exclaimed. "I am far from such an idea. The impressions made at school certainly become effaced; even the most impressionable may become accomplished wives and excellent mothers."

"Then some may escape the bad impressions of which you speak, and leave school as pure as when they entered it?"

"Undoubtedly," she replied. "It depends entirely on the companions they associate with."

The turn our coversation had taken appeared to have awakened in her some distant recollections. With her elbow on the table, her head supported by her hand, she was silent for a few moments. Suddenly, without changing her attitude, her eyes still lowered, she went on in a low voice, as if speaking to herself.

"At fourteen the mind is already awakened (but for coquetry only, a sort of instinctive coquetry in women); it is free from all stain, owing to the maternal education received until then. Suddenly we are sent away to school. We are chilled, a sentiment of solitude invades us, we are lost among all those strangers who stare at us without uttering a word; at recreation we run to hide in a corner to think of the little room so dear to us, of the home where we have spent so many happy days, and cherished ones we have left there. 'Oh! how sad my mother must be,' we cry. 'I am sure she must be weeping at this moment,' and we burst into tears at the remembrance of those she shed when we tore ourselves from her arms.

"Raising the head, we discover that we are not alone on the bench on which we have taken refuge. A young girl of about the same age is seated there also.

"'Do not weep,' she says, taking possession of one hand, 'you will not be unhappy here; you will find that we amuse ourselves well sometimes. Where do you come from? Have you ever been away to school before?'

"Happy in having some one to speak to, we immediately make her a confidante.

"Little by little we learn to love each other with all our souls. Sympathy soon wins a heart of fourteen when surrounded by strangers. Oh! if it were a man who said: 'What a pretty figure you have, I love your eyes, your hands are charming—let me admire them.' We would instinctively blush, run away to escape such compliments. But when it is a young girl who speaks, we listen untroubled, often with pleasure, and compliment her in turn.

"From compliment to compliment, confidence to confidence, our companion acquires influence; she has been there for many years, we have been there but a month or two, she knows the ways of the place and willingly initiates us, at the same time she is more matured, more experienced; she places her experience at our service, at an age when we ask but to be instructed.

"Soon it is not merely affection we feel for her, but fear and respect; we are so ignorant, so small beside her. She has reached this point by winning our confidence, by exercising a kind of slow and continued pressure on our mind, obliging us to see through her, taking away from us the consciousness of right and wrong, dominating and bending us to her caprices.

"Sometimes we try to shake off the yoke; it is impossible; a thousand indissoluble links, a thousand tyrannical thoughts chain us until we leave school. At this time only, the links are broken, the recollections effaced—unless," she added lowering her voice, "hazard, or rather fatality reunites us again, and then—"

"Then?" I asked.

"Then, we are lost," she murmured.

"What! you believe one cannot escape the influence you speak of?" I cried.

"Perhaps—with time and distance," she replied.

You see, my dear friend, she had reached the point where she judged her past existence and condemned it without having received one reproach from me. I assure you that she spoke in all sincerity, with no intention of inspiring a confidence which she would abuse later, or of making me conceive a better opinion of her. She had really entered into a new path, with that earnestness and relative frankness which you must have recognized in her if I have painted her character truly. But as she admitted herself, time alone could maintain her in this path, strengthen her resolutions, efface the first impressions from her mind and render it inaccessible to the influence so long exercised over it. Alas! I was too happy over the results obtained to trouble myself about the future; time would come to my aid; of that I could not doubt. What event, what accident could disturb the work that was being accomplished? Our retreat was ignored by all, and Paule herself had not the faintest idea of the whereabouts of the one who alone in the world possessed enough influence over her mind to take her from the right path.

Full of confidence in a happier future, persuaded that my fate depended on myself, and that my long cherished dreams would soon be realized, I was no longer nervous and impatient as in other days; my love was more tranquil. It was even in some measure transformed; I now looked on Paule as if she were a sick child whom it was my duty to nurse back to health. I had become enamored of my task as a physician becomes attached to a patient who has been condemned by his colleagues, and whom he hopes to save; as the chaplain of a prison becomes attached to the criminal whom his exhortations have brought back to repentance. My love was becoming more immaterial; I had less desire and more tenderness. Paule seemed deeply touched by my care and delicate attentions; she often thanked me by a smile, a glance, or a pressure of the hand. I even remarked that she was becoming a little coquettish with me, no doubt through a spirit of opposition.

As you see, my dear friend, I am nearing my aim, and you have no doubt that I will attain it. I thank you for this proof of confidence, but before you rejoice over my happiness, pray turn the page of this manuscript.

XX

During our stay at Oran I arose early every morning and took a long ride on horseback while Paule still slept or dressed. Ben-Kader watched for my return and as soon as he caught sight of me went in and informed my wife. She would immediately come down and we would then enter the carriage which was brought every day at ten o'clock to convey us to the Queen's Bath.

One morning—it was a Saturday I believe—as I reached the hotel, Ben-Kader came to meet me and placed himself in front of my horse.

"You know, you, the lady, she is gone!" he said in a sad tone.

"What lady?" I asked, puzzled.

"Your lady."

"Gone where?" I asked, alighting from my horse.

"Over there," he said, gravely stretching his arm in the direction of the sea.

I started, but immediately recovered myself. Had I not seen Paule that very morning, before mounting my horse, and had she not told me to come back as soon as possible! Weary of waiting, she had no doubt gone for a walk in the direction of the harbor; that must be what the yaouley meant. As I entered the hotel, I met a waiter.

"Has my wife gone out?" I asked without attaching much importance to the question.

"Yes, monsieur, she went out an hour ago with another lady who called a few moments after you had gone this morning."

"A lady! what lady?" I repeated, a terrible suspicion flashing through my mind.

"I do not know, monsieur; I have never seen her in Oran; she is a stranger!"

"Ah! a stranger! A Frenchwoman, you mean."

"She may be; at any rate, she is a foreigner."

"And that lady," I rejoined, trembling, "is no doubt young, pretty and a blonde?"

"Oh! no, monsieur; she is about forty and she has black hair."

I breathed again.

"She appeared to me," added the waiter, to be a lady's maid."

He had scarcely pronounced these words when I left him precipitately. I rushed to our apartments and entered Paule's room.

Nothing announced a departure; her dresses were hanging in their habitual place, her linen was arranged in the drawers, her trunk was still in the same corner. Evidently, my fears were groundless; she had gone out with some person of the town, a shop-woman, probably, and would soon return.

I returned to the parlor, which I had merely crossed and approached the chimney to see the time. A paper placed in front of the clock attracted my attention. It was a note written hurriedly by Paule, and contained these few words:

"I am obliged to leave you for a few days. Forgive me and be patient. I will return, I swear it."

I took no time to reflect on the meaning of the note; I understood but one thing: she was gone, and I must overtake her at any cost. I rushed down-stairs, crossed the vestibule, and as I stepped out my eyes fell on Ben-Kader dozing quietly on the walk.

"Come," I cried, "lead me!"

"Where?" he asked.

"You told me my wife had gone; what direction did she take?"

He did not answer but walked gravely in front of me in the direction of the port. I urged and begged him to walk faster, but all in vain; he was not to be hurried. At last he stopped before a house on the quay and silently pointed to a poster on which I read the following notice.

"The Steamer Oasis, Captain Raoul will sail at ten o'clock to-day, Saturday, for Gibraltar."

I turned to Ben-Kader. He extended his arm in the direction of the sea and said in a mournful voice, with tears in his eyes:

"Very far."

This pantomime was as eloquent as the longest discourse. Paule had embarked at ten o'clock for Gibraltar, and twelve had just struck. I was asking myself what I should do when I was accosted by an official of the Steamship Company whom I had met at the Cafe Soubiran.

"What!" he cried, "are you here! I thought you had gone with your wife. I saw her embark this morning on the Oasis and I supposed you were already on board."

"There is some misunderstanding," I replied, "I am trying to find some means of reaching Gibraltar as soon as possible."

"The deuce! I know of none. The next steamer sails next Saturday?"

"Could I not go to Carthagena and from there to Gibraltar?"

"The service is interrupted just now."

"Could I not find some means of crossing the strait? Think of my wife's anxiety!"

"I understand that, but the boats from Oran do not undertake such long trips. Ah! if you were only at Nemours—"

"At Nemours? Can I not get there?"

"It is quite a distance."

"How many leagues?"

"Fifty by the Tlemcen route; thirty by following the coast."

"Can it be followed?"

"Yes, on horseback, if that does not frighten you."

"I lived in Egypt a long time and I am used to such expeditions."

"Then I shall trace your itinerary?"

"You would oblige me very much."

"You will engage a *calechier* to conduct you to Andalousis in three hours. From there you will go to Bou-Sfeur and stop at the house of a Spanish farmer, Peres-Antonio. You will ask for a guide and horses. He will procure them for you if you tell him you come from me."

"I shall not fail to do so."

"When you reach Nemours, you will send for the owner of a *balancelle* while you rest at the hotel. A *balancelle* is quite a stanch craft, half-decked, and manned by two or three men. It transports fruit from Gibraltar to Nemours and returns with a load of coral. For a few louis you can engage immediate passage and if the wind is favorable you will reach your destination about twelve hours after the steamer that left this morning."

"I will not lose an instant!" I cried, and thanking him warmly, I hurried away.

At half-past twelve I was on the road to Nemours. Ben-Kader begged to be allowed to accompany me, but I feared a voyage by sea for this child, habituated to terra firma, and refused his sevices. Fatality pursued me; I am now convinced that if I had yielded to the yaouley's prayers, my expedition would have turned out differently. You will know why, later.

I believe you are not astonished, my friend, by my obstinacy in following my wife, not-withstanding the difficulty of the pursuit and the promise contained in the note she had left behind. You must already share my suspicions and terrors; the person with whom Paule had left in the morning could be none other but Mme. de Blangy's maid, the same who on the evening of our departure from Paris, had spoken to my wife through the carriage window. But how had this woman come to Oran? How had she learned our presence in that town? It mattered little. It was evident she had been dispatched by Mme. de Blangy. The latter must have escaped from her husband and waited for Paule in Gibraltar. The first thing was to overtake them; then decide what I should do.

XXI

I will not give you the details of that wild chase—they are effaced from my memory. I traversed villages, arid plains, rivers, forests, and my guide, though an Arab, found it difficult to follow me. Thanks to the excellent directions I had received, I reached Nemours in the night. To think that if I had been less hurried, if instead of entering Nemours while its inhabitants were sleeping, I had wandered through its streets in broad daylight, I—an instant more and you will understand.

I alighted from my horse, and without thinking of rest, directed my steps toward the port. I entered an inn which sheltered many sailors every night, and soon secured my passage for Gibraltar from the owner of a *balancelle*. We set sail at sunrise; I wrapped my cloak about me, stretched myself in the stern near the rudder and found some rest from my fatigues.

The weather was favorable. We crossed quickly and without incident. When I reached Gibraltar, I learned that the Oasis, which had entered port the previous day, had not yet departed. I immediately went in search of Captain Raoul, a charming man, whom Paule and myself had met many times at dinner at the Hotel de la Paix. He was on board, and greeted me almost in the same terms as the official at Oran.

"What! you here!" he cried, as soon as he recognized me.

"Certainly," I replied, "is it not natural that I should rejoin my wife? I missed the Oasis; she must have told you."

"No, indeed; she told me, on the contrary, that you preferred going to Nemours by land; as she was not afraid of the sea, she took passage with her maid and enjoyed the voyage."

"Where is she now?" I asked.

"Well," laughed the captain, "you must be playing hide-and-seek. You give each other rendezvous at Nemours, your wife stops there and during that time—"

"What!" I cried, "the Oasis stopped at Nemours?"

"Why, we stop there whenever the weather permits; we left more than ten passengers there this trip."

"And my wife was of the number?"

"Why certainly, my dear monsieur. Really, decidedly, I don't understand."

But alas! I understood, and that was sufficient. I had traversed the Mediterranean in a *balancelle* to learn that my wife was at Nemours. I was promenading in Spain while she had remained in the province of Oran. The previous day, I had no doubt passed through the street where she was; I had perhaps stopped before her door to ask for information. Ah! if only, as I said a few moments ago, I had been wise enough to await daylight, if even I had taken Ben-Kader with me he would have guessed that she was in the town, or at least, during our run on horseback he would have found the opportunity to tell me, that the Oasis touched on the coast before crossing. The official at Oran had not given me this information, thinking it useless as the ship would touch at Nemours many hours before I could reach it.

I must now retrace my steps. The Oasis would not return for three days, and Captain Raoul advised me to return by the *balancelle* that had brought me to Gibraltar. I followed his advice. But the wind which had favored me when I was drifting away from Paule, became contrary when I was returning to her; even the elements conspired against me. After a most tedious voyage, I reached Nemours one week after I had left it. I obtained, without difficulty, all the information I desired concerning Paule. I was shown the house where she had stopped with one of her friends—a Frenchwoman who had waited there some time for her and departed with her the day following my passage through Nemours. The two travelers, accompanied by a maid, had gone in the direction of Oran by the Tlemcen route; they must have reached there at least five days ago.

Can you believe it, my dear friend? I did not hasten to rejoin them. During the past week, anger, indignation, the ardor of the struggle, had sustained me. Now, my nerves were distended, emotion succeeded anger, and I succumbed under a weight of moral and physical lassitude.

"Why should I hurry," I said to myself; "hazard leads me on, fatality pursues me."

I abandoned the reins on my horse's neck and let him go as he pleased. Softly rocked on my saddle, my eyes half closed, I had strange hallucinations; I heard Madame de Blangy's voice reproaching Paule for having followed me, for having remained so long at Oran without trying to rejoin her.

"You prefer him to me now," she said; "his affection has replaced mine. But I will tear you from his love. We shall fly far, far away, where we cannot be found."

"No!" cried Paule, "go, leave me. You have been my ruin. I must rejoin him—he taught me honesty, duty; he awaits me, he suffers, he calls me. I go—"

"Well then, I go with you. But if he did not wait for you, it is because he does not love you, because he has deceived you, and then I shall take you away with me."

I saw them arriving in Oran, Paule rushing to the hotel; I was not there. Then Madame de Blangy became more pressing; she spoke of their ten years of friendship, the promises of their school-days later renewed; she evoked all the feelings that united them; she magnetized her by her words, riveted a new ring in the long chain of their intrigues and dragged her far away from me, distracted, dying.

This is what I heard, this is what I saw in that return run of thirty leagues through the desert, and this is what awaited me in Oran. A letter from Paule; I copy it literally:

"I am a wretched creature. But I must tell you what has passed. I do not want you to accuse me of falsehood and duplicity. You have enough else to reproach me. I was sincere and true during my sojourn here; keep at least this remembrance of me.

"As we were leaving Rue Caumartin, her maid stealthily came to me and said: 'Madame goes with her husband; she knows that you are leaving also, and has ordered me to reassure and follow you.' This maid took the express that conveyed us to Marseilles; but at the moment of our embarkation she disappeared, and had I not been persuaded that she had lost trace of us, I would have asked you to leave Oran two months ago. I swear it.

"As to *her*, while in Ireland, she evaded her husband's surveillance, escaped, joined her maid in Paris, who informed her of our whereabouts; she then departed immediately, traversed France, Spain, the Mediterranean, and landed at Nemours. There she wrote, imploring me to come to her; she said she was ill, and promised to retain me but one day. After a long resistance I left, swearing to return to you. I kept my oath, returned with the intention of taking shelter with you, of imploring your aid and protection against myself. But I did not find you. Ah! why did you not wait? Why have you abandoned me? left me to her mercy—I, who am so weak, so cowardly, when she is near? You scorn me—you despise me! You have no wish to see me again. Ah! I understand you—I understand you; and yet I was becoming better—I swear it. I was beginning a new life; a great change was taking place within me. But it had not yet time to complete itself; I was not yet strong enough, purified enough, regenerated enough, to resist bad advice. Have I not admitted what influence she possesses over me? how she dominates and enslaves me? I did not want to go; I wanted to wait for you; but you did not return. I knew not what had become of you. Then, I was afraid of you, and said to myself: 'Will he forgive me?' I dared not hope for it—and she! always near me, always at my side, reproaching my weakness, my cowardice, saying—oh! I will not repeat it, I should not even speak of her to you!

"At last she has decided me: I go—I go where she leads me; I know not where! What matters where I hide my shame? I am a fallen, lost creature—I am less than nothing, and I shall never rise. As you see, you have undertaken an impossible task; we deluded ourselves. It is better it should end thus. I have ruined your life. You, who are so good, so noble, so upright! Do not search for me; you will never find me. She will hide me better than you have done. Besides, I do not want to see you again. I would not dare look at you, speak to you—to act thus, when you have been so generous to me! Ah! why have you not again spoken of your love since we came here? There was no longer a bolt on my door. But my past was against me—you still scorned me, and I was waiting until time should have regenerated me—until I should be worthy of you. Oh! what a mistake we have made! To-day there would be between us indissoluble links that no one could break. Adieu, adieu; forget me, pity me. Ah! if you should return while I write this letter. I would throw myself at your feet, I—there; I will wait until to-morrow—say what she may, I will not leave until to-morrow. But come—come quickly!"

She had reopened her letter and added these few words:

"I have waited two days more. What has become of you? You have returned to France; you have abandoned me. I go. Adieu! adieu!"

I reread this letter two or three times mechanically. I was stupefied; I felt pain throughout my whole body; my head was heavy, my teeth were chattering.

I took my bed; a violent fever, accompanied by delirium, took possession of me during the night. In the morning, as I did not go down, the host came to my apartments, and hastily sent for Doctor X. For many days he despaired of my recovery, but he at last triumphed over the disease—typhoid fever, I believe.

The first part of January I was able to return to France. I was still very weak physically, but my long illness had rested me mentally. There had been a stoppage of time in my life, a sort of suspension of animation which was salutary to me. I remembered all the events that had taken place, but I thought of them without bitterness, without irritation, only with a great sadness. I suffered much, but my pain had nothing of sharpness. It was latent; it smoldered like a fire covered with ashes; it burned, but made no flame.

Nevertheless, I experienced a deep emotion when I re-entered my apartments in the Rue Caumartin. A thousand recollections assailed me; I wept long—very long.

When I became stronger, I collected all that had belonged to Paule, and sent it to her mother. At the same time I wrote this to M. Giraud:

"Your daughter has left me, monsieur. I do not know where she has taken refuge, and I do not want to know. Pray never question me on the subject. You will understand me that I wish to forget."

I knew that M. de Blangy was in Paris, but I made no attempt to see him, and he had the same reserve.

One day, however, we met on the boulevards; he came to me and grasped my hand warmly.

"I am happy to find you in good health," he said; "I feared you were ill."

"I have been seriously ill," I replied. "I am better—in every way. And you?"

"I have never been better in my life."

We were then silent for a few moments; The comte was the first to speak.

"It would, perhaps, be wiser not to speak of the past," he said, "but you must admit that it is difficult to avoid it. Between us, all conversation bearing no reference to—our adventures would be impossible."

"Then let us speak of the situation frankly."

"What an unfortunate campaign we have made!"

"Very unfortunate."

"She rejoined you?"

"Yes, in Africa. I had not foreseen that she would send her maid to follow us."

I related all the details of my voyage and sojourn in Oran. I then summed up Paule's letter in a few words.

"Yes," he said, after listening attentively to me, "your wife is better than mine. But then, that is not a very great merit."

He then related the incidents of his own journey in the north of Europe.

"When Mme. de Blangy realized that she had to follow me," he said in a careless tone, which left no doubt in my mind of his recovery, "she accepted the inevitable gracefully. 'What an excellent idea of yours to return,' she said at each instant. 'How amiable of you! I desired so much to travel! We are then going to the north? How delighted I am! Why did you not think of this before? I am so tired of Paris. But do you know, my dear, that your wanderings through the world have benefited you? You have grown young; one would scarcely give you thirty years. Indeed, I am falling in love with you once more!'

"I might have believed she was telling the truth," continued the comte, "if I had not long known her to be the most false of women, and if I had not guessed that she was playing a part. Would you like to know her game? We have no secrets for each other, and besides, I have no reason to spare the creature who has no claims upon me. She played the role of Delilah toward Samson. During the whole journey she saturated me with her love, that she might deliver me into the hands of the Philistines; that is, escape without being pursued. With her quick wit, she soon understood that I no longer loved her—that it was not my heart that had prompted me to return, but that my imagination, still excited by an abruptly interrupted liaison, needed to be soothed.

"Madame de Blangy had enough suppleness of mind to calm the most exalted imagination. She succeeded well with mine. When she left me one night in Dublin, I assure you that I experienced such great relief that I would not have dreamed of pursuing her, had I not remembered the engagement contracted with you. This engagement it was impossible for me to carry out, and you will laugh at the trick she played me; it was worthy of her. She carried away my purse with her, and I found myself without a sou. I was obliged to write to France for funds. I received them a week later, on the same day I received my purse. Mme. de Blangy returned it without opening it—I must do her this justice. That was equivalent to telling me that she was in safety, and I could now follow her if I desired. I may have been guilty of a little indifference, it is true. But pray forgive me; I had not the courage to struggle any longer. The idea of this double expedition was yours. I do not reproach you, but allow me to say that it was not a happy one.

"I have resumed my occupations in Paris, and if some day a colleague or club associate has the temerity to remind me that there still exists a Madame de Blangy, I will have the honor of immediately sending him my seconds. Two or three affairs of the kind will suffice to convince all my acquaintances that I am a widower. If you will permit me, in taking leave of you, my dear monsieur, to give you a word of advice, I will say; treat your friends in the same manner."

A FEW DAYS AFTER THIS conversation, my dear friend, I had the pleasure of meeting you at the reception of the Rue Friedland.

At that time I was anxious for distractions and, as I wrote you at the time, I hoped that the bustle and movement would bring some diversion to my melancholy. But the day following that fete I felt more sad, more discouraged than ever. I had not the strength to meet you at the appointed rendezvous, and I left on a trip that very day.

One morning, shortly after my return to Paris, in the month of June, one of the servants announced Mme. Giraud.

"Tell her to come in," I said, after a moment of hesitation.

"You have begged my husband to never speak of our daughter in your presence," said Paule's mother when she had seated herself. "We have respected your wishes, and wept in silence over the misfortune that has befallen all. We would still continue to do so, if it were not a question of fulfilling a promise torn from us. Paule is ill—very ill—almost dying. She has begged us to tell you this, and to implore you to see her once more."

When I could control my emotion, I asked Mme. Giraud if Paule was in Paris.

"No," she said, wiping away her tears, "she is in Z—, a small village on the coast of Normandy. It can be reached in a few hours."

"I will go," I replied simply.

Mme. Giraud rushed to me, grasped my hands, and cried:

"Oh! thank you, thank you! What joy you will cause her! I know not what fault she has committed toward you; I saw her again only three days ago. Somebody wrote that she was very ill and I hastened to her; a mother cannot help forgiving her dying child. She did not tell me the cause of your separation—indeed, she had not the strength, and moreover, I had not the courage to question her. But I understood from her desire to see you, and her repentance, that all the blame was on her side. Oh! forgive her, monsieur, forgive her! Give her that consolation before she dies!"

"But are you not exaggerating the situation!" I cried. "Is there no hope of saving her?"

"No," she replied; "I had a conversation with the physician, who was summoned from Paris. He did not know I was her mother, and told me the truth. She is attacked by a cerebral malady, of which I have forgotten the name."

"*Pachy-meningite*," I said mechanically, suddenly remembering the terrible prognostication of Doctor X—.

"Yes, that is it," said the poor woman. "Her memory is becoming weaker day by day; her ideas are no longer clear; she can scarcely find the words to express herself. During the night she is plunged in a stupor which is not sleep and in which she hears voices that threaten her. She is extremely weak; yesterday, to reassure me she tried to raise herself from her couch but her limbs refused to support her."

The poor woman stopped, choked by her sobs. When she had grown more calm I promised to leave that very day, and asked her for the necessary directions to find the house in which Paule was living.

"Before reaching Z—," she said, "at a short distance from the village, you will ask for Madame de Blangy's cottage."

"Madame de Blangy!" I exclaimed, unable to repress my indignation. She looked at me, thought she understood, and said:

"You are angry with her, no doubt; she was my daughter's friend, and should have advised her. She may not have known, however; there are certain secrets which we do not confide even to our most intimate friends. But let not this prevent you from keeping your promise. You will not meet Madame de Blangy. I did not see her once during my stay at Z—. She avoided me, and will no doubt avoid you also."

As soon as Mme. Giraud had gone, I prepared for departure. The next morning, after a night in a railway carriage, I took a cab and was conveyed to Z—.

The cottage in which Madame de Blangy had buried herself in solitude with Paule nestled on a hillside, and was sheltered by the cliffs. The coachman pointed it out to me. I alighted, and to avoid all awkward meetings, I sent an urchin to announce my arrival to my wife. A quarter of an hour later I was at her side.

Mme. Giraud had not exaggarated. Paule was very ill. She however had strength to extend an emaciated hand, on which I pressed my lips, and to say:

"I am glad you came to-day—to-morrow it would have been too late."

The effort exhausted her; she closed her eyes. I contemplated her in silence; she was but the shadow of herself. I had not believed she could have changed as much. My tears dropped on her hands. She felt that I was weeping, and murmured, "Thank you."

At each instant her lips opened, and I thought she would speak, but the words would not come. During the night she was a prey to the hallucinations of which her mother had spoken. She appeared to be struggling against a phantom which she tried to push away with her hands, and which returned incessantly. Hoarse cries escaped from her throat, and sometimes by bending over her, I heard her mutter disjointed phrases like these:

"Go away! go away! Wretch! Lost! I am afraid, I am afraid! Him! him!"

In the morning she was calmer. Seated in her reclining-chair in front of the window, she opened her eyes now and then and looked far away over the sea. Once I thought the light fatigued her, and I advanced toward the window to draw the curtains. She saw my movement, and I heard her murmur:

"No, no! Leave it. This view does me good. I imagine myself still over there, far away over there, near you, at Oran."

Toward noon her mother arrived from Paris, accompanied by the doctor, who had come to Z—three days previous. He approached the patient, thought he noticed some improvement, and inquired if she had taken some nourishment according to his instructions.

"A little broth only," he was told.

"It is not enough," he said; "she must take something strengthening. If between now and evening this improvement continues, we must try to give her some substantial food, which I shall prepare myself."

When the physician had gone, Paule beckoned me to her. I obeyed.

"He is right," she said; "I feel better today. How kind you are to come! Two months ago, when I was taken ill, I wanted to write to you, but I did not dare. I acted so badly. Ah! I am well punished—well punished. Forgive me." She stopped, but resumed in a few seconds: "You will not leave me—you will remain here near me, with my mother. You will let no one come in. If I die you must take my body to Paris. I don't want it to be buried here. Oh, no! Oh, no!"

A few minutes after this I heard some noise in the next room, and turned abruptly. She saw my movement and said:

"Do not fear; she will not dare come. I have forbidden her. If I could not live near you, I will at least die in your arms."

About five o'clock we thought it time to obey the doctor's directions, and offered her the food he had prepared. We expected she would refuse it; but a phenomenon, often observed in the malady of which Paule was the victim, now presented itself. Her appetite was suddenly reanimated; she eagerly took the food and carried it quickly to her mouth.

But it stopped in the paralyzed œsophagus. The eyes became injected with blood, the face took on a purple hue. She died—asphyxiated.

In accordance with her expressed wish, I took her body to Paris, and she was buried three days later in Pere-Lachaise.

One morning, in the month of September of the same year, M. de Blangy read with deep interest the following paragraph in a newspaper:

"The little village of Z—was yesterday the scene of a highly dramatic tragedy. A charming woman of the best society, and an intrepid swimmer, the Countess de Blangy, who has been spending the summer at that place, was returning from an excursion on the cliffs, in company with her friend, Mlle. B—, the ravishing young brunette, who attracted so much attention at the last ball of the Casino, when the idea suddenly came to her to go in bathing. Her friend observed that the tide was going out, and that the currents, which are very violent at this season, might carry her out to sea; beside, there were no good swimmers on the beach at that moment to go to her aid in case of danger.

"'Never mind,' said the countess, 'I can take care of myself.'

"She entered one of the cottages, and soon came out in an elegant bathing costume. In a few strokes she was swimming in deep water.

"'Come back! come back!' cried everybody from the beach.

"She paid no heed to these cries, but continued to swim, now and then bursting into peals of laughter that reassured her friends. Soon, however, the spectators realized that she was being carried out by the undertow.

"'Help! help!' cried Mlle. B—, wildly.

"At this moment M. Adrien de C— appeared on the scene, and was soon informed of what was taking place.

"'Ah, it is Madame de Blangy,' he exclaimed, as he hastily prepared to go to her rescue. The woman he was trying to save at the peril of his own life was the intimate friend of the young wife, whom he lost last

June, and whom he still mourns so deeply that he cannot tear himself away from the vicinity.

"He soon reached Mme. de Blangy. Notwithstanding the distance their efforts could be distinctly seen. A struggle seemed to be taking place between them. Like all drowning persons, Mme. de Blangy was, no doubt, making desperate efforts to clutch her savior, and the latter pushed her back that he might be free in his movements. The current still dragged them out, and they were soon lost to view.

"Ten minutes glided by—a century! M. Adrien de C— reappeared. Alas! he was alone. He had been unable to save the unfortunate woman, and had scarcely enough strength left to reach the beach."

AFTER READING THIS ACCOUNT, M. de Blangy took his pen and wrote:

"I understand, and thank you in my name and in the name of all honest people, for having ridden us of this reptile. The danger you have run absolves you."

He folded this letter and sent it to M Adrien de C—, Rue Caumartin.

THE END

A Note About the Author

Adolphe Belot (1829–1890) was a French novelist and playwright. Born in Pointe-à-Pitre, Guadeloupe, Belot was raised in Le Havre, where he followed in his father's footsteps to become a lawyer. After joining the board of lawyers of Nancy, Belot traveled to the Americas, where he became inspired to pursue a career as a professional writer. After writing several successful plays, including *Le Testament de César Girodot* (1859), Belot published the novel *Mademoiselle Giraud, My Wife* (1870). An immediate commercial and critical success, the novel earned Belot a reputation as a leading popular writer in France and around the world.

A Note from the Publisher

Spanning many genres, from non-fiction essays to literature classics to children's books and lyric poetry, Mint Edition books showcase the master works of our time in a modern new package. The text is freshly typeset, is clean and easy to read, and features a new note about the author in each volume. Many books also include exclusive new introductory material. Every book boasts a striking new cover, which makes it as appropriate for collecting as it is for gift giving. Mint Edition books are only printed when a reader orders them, so natural resources are not wasted. We're proud that our books are never manufactured in excess and exist only in the exact quantity they need to be read and enjoyed. To learn more and view our library, go to minteditionbooks.com

CPSIA information can be obtained
at www.ICGtesting.com
Printed in the USA
BVHW041711010421
603943BV00008B/106

9 781513 295381